CLIFF EDGE

FLORRIE PALMER

Print ISBN 978-1-913419-86-8

ALSO BY FLORRIE PALMER

The Decoy

For my children and grandchildren with so much love.

PROLOGUE

Dwarfed by the wild north Pembrokeshire scenery and the scale of the massive cliffs, two figures battled against what had become a strong north-easterly wind. Kinder when they had set out, the weather had worsened. Their trekking poles were little help on the rocky surface of the cliff path as it descended toward the collapsed sea cave. The vast, noisy Atlantic drove its angry passage past Ireland to merge with the Irish Sea and smash against the cliff walls below.

The couple made slow progress until one of them stopped, seeming to want to turn back. The one in front appeared to remonstrate and urge the other forward. Tentatively, the two picked their way downhill until they reached a precarious, bridge-like arch that crossed a huge blowhole in the grassed clifftop. Coral-billed choughs cawed and flew off their rock perches as the people approached.

Water surged through the sea-tunnel into the pool below and monstrous sucking sounds emanated from the raging waves as they entered the cave, flinging volumes of surf high into the air. Awestruck by the seething sight below, the pair stood gazing down. Above, hovering seagulls watched one of them stumble, lose their footing and lurch forward. In a useless attempt to maintain balance, their arms flailed as their terrified scream was drowned by the howl and roar of the wind and sea.

On its way to meet death, the falling body did not hear the edge of triumph in the voice of the other as it cut through the air, 'Happy New Year!'

1

3 JANUARY 2018. LLANGUNNOR, CARMARTHEN, WALES

DCI Jane Owen gets up a little later than usual. She's on from 0830 today. Apart from road accidents – of which there were always more than usual in icy conditions – there are few incidents requiring police attention. Crime seems to slow down, and people are not keen to go out to commit theft or get up to no good in weather like they've been having, so there's not a lot going on for her at the moment. But then you never know. She rubs the sand out of her eyes and yawns one more time before jumping out of bed and reaching for her fleecy dressing gown and fluffy slippers. She shuffles to the bathroom where she showers and performs the usual morning requisites. Today, she decides to wear the navy wool office trouser suit with the cream polo neck underneath. That should keep her warm over the thermal long johns and vest. The station heating is unreliable at best.

Returning to her bedroom, she dresses before sitting down at her small, messy dressing table. Watching herself in the mirror, she combs her thick, short, straight brown hair back from her face, but it is so floppy that it won't be long before it's worked its way forward again so she has to tuck it behind pretty, neat little ears. She cut off her longer locks a while back. Nowadays, her life needs to be as easy as she can make it and she doesn't have time for getting long hair to look good. She still misses it but doesn't think she looks too bad with it short.

She is new to her position and wants to look as good as she can in the role so takes care over her appearance.

Dotting two right-hand fingers with foundation, she circles and spreads it carefully to cover her long, intelligent face. Mascara is brushed onto the long lashes that surround her doe-like brown eyes and from a small selection of colours, she carefully chooses a pale-pink lipstick to paint her small mouth. Slipping on her flat, black fur-lined boots, she is now in her 'battle dress'. She'll be driving to the station today –far too cold to walk. Smacking her lips together, she checks her face one last time before leaving her bedroom.

She crosses the small kitchen where she draws back the curtains, opens the window to the silent, frozen morning and calls, 'Ma-a-army!'

Quickly closing the window, she looks across the front garden that slopes down to the road with its scattering of a few other bungalows either side, beyond which the whitened land rises high to frosted hills. The weather is still at sub-zero but at least it has stopped snowing for the moment, although the white blanket of sky augurs more to come. There's already been more than enough and it's time it stopped now.

A ginger cat hurtles through the cat flap. Making voracious mewing sounds as it pads across the floor to her feet, it rubs an icy cheek against Jane's ankles and executes a sensual circle of her lower legs, the furry body and tail transferring its chill and some hairs to her trousers. Jane moves her legs out of the way and bends to give the animal a quick stroke. 'Nobbling out, is it?'

The cat arches its spine. *Amazing,* she thinks, *how these animals don't seem to mind the cold, especially since they love the warmth so much.* She bends to open a cupboard from which she takes a tin of cat food from a box of six. She peels back the lid and throws it in the swing bin. Glancing at her watch, she thinks she should probably hurry. She takes the fork left ready on the worktop beside the cat bowl and dollops half the tinned meat into it, then covers the half-filled tin with the plastic lid also left ready and puts it in the refrigerator. She places the bowl on the floor. The purring cat gobbles it down.

Returning to the bathroom, Jane unhooks a plastic kitchen apron from the back of the door, picks up the washing-up bowl from its place beside the basin pedestal, puts it in the bath under the taps and half-fills it with warm water into which she adds some soap bubbles and drops the big pink sponge. She dons the apron then takes a towel from the rail and drapes it over her arm. Then she carries the bowl to a bedroom door, grips it carefully with one hand, knocking loudly with the other before opening it and entering the room. She flicks the light switch by the door and walks carefully to the bedside where she places the bowl on the floor. She's glad they bought this place a few years ago. It works for Meg and is so much easier for them both. She is now so close to work she can walk if she feels like it.

The lilt in her voice is like a soft morning song. 'Hello, lovely, how did you sleep?'

Half awake, Meg mumbles into her pillow. But she seems okay so Jane doesn't waste time. She gives her sister a hand to lift herself up into a sitting position and prop herself against the bedhead.

'Arms up, darling.'

Meg is twenty-two years old and taller than her sister who is ten years her senior. Extremely young to be in the position she is, Jane has fast-tracked her way in the department and there is a certain resentment amongst some of her elders, of which she is painfully aware.

Meg raises her left arm and with shaky difficulty only manages to raise the other about halfway up. Jane peels the nightie over her sleepy head then deftly takes the plastic nappy changer from the bedside cupboard, unrolls and places it on the edge of the bed as close to the girl's hips as possible. With one practised arm, she lifts and rolls Meg towards her while the other feeds the changer under her bottom.

Now awake, Meg pinches her sister's bum as she bends to the bowl to squeeze the warm wet sponge. Jane pinches her sister's forearm in retaliation. The sisters have a special relationship that has become more than its genetic origin. They are in turn each other's mothers, daughters, closest friends and at times, though fortunately seldom, each other's worst enemies. They have reached a stage where words are often not necessary to convey their thoughts to one another – almost as if they were identical twins in spite of their ten years and biological differences. They have also now reached a stage when neither can imagine life without the other.

There is a special lift for the bath but that is only used once a week when there is the luxury of time. Jane passes the sponge to Meg who washes and towels her top half first and her groin. Then she pulls the changer down and hastily washes the withered, useless legs before drying them and dressing Meg in some clothing they had agreed the night before: loose knickers and black elastic-waisted trousers draped on the back of the chair beside the bed.

Jane hands Meg a roll-on deodorant, a blue shirt and thick blue cardigan. Her sister leans herself forward and puts on the deodorant and clothes by herself. They never chatter much at this hour, both being slow wake-uppers and natural night owls. It always takes a cup of tea for Meg and coffee for Jane to properly come to life.

Jane crosses the room, pulls back the curtains and brings the wheelchair over to the bed and puts on the brakes so that it can't move about. Now comes the tricky bit. Meg swivels herself onto the side of the bed in readiness for Jane's help. Jane dresses the dangling feet in socks and cosy fur-lined slippers. Her least liked task. Paralysed feet are not obliging and do not stay put.

That done, she half-lifts Meg onto the chair. A small-framed woman, Jane stands five feet four and weighs only nine stone. But she's wiry, strong and has a determined nature, like Meg who once in the chair, takes over and wheels herself through to the bathroom. The self-propelling wheelchair has a commode in the seat, so if needs must Meg can use it. Usually she can hang on till Carys arrives and helps her to the toilet, but not always. The bathroom is wheelchair friendly, but she doesn't yet have the strength to lift herself from the chair onto the adapted toilet. Through physiotherapy Meg has developed good strength in her left arm, but although it is slowly improving, her right only has just enough to help propel herself forward. The wheelchair has a habit of veering to the right on account of this imbalance.

A physiotherapist still visits fortnightly and the arm and hand exercises are ongoing but torn nerves take a long time to recover. Meg still has to lift her mobile to her ear with the left hand. It is hoped that in time she will regain full use of the right arm. Luckily, the young woman has a positive spirit and tries hard to keep cheerful.

Jane follows her into the bathroom, carefully lets down one arm of the chair so that she can help slide and lift Meg onto the high, wide-seated toilet, then leaves her to it, the sliding door slightly open. She goes to the kitchen and flips the already half-filled kettle on. Opening the fridge, she pulls out the sliced, brown sourdough bread and slots one piece into the toaster. Taking out a small jug of milk, the packet of low-fat spread and a probiotic drink, she places them where Meg can reach them.

Some time ago, she discovered through trial and error that it is easier to prepare as much as she can of breakfast the night before. The little blue-and-white-stripy teapot waits on a circular laminated mat on the table with a tea bag already in it for Meg. Two matching breakfast bowls and mugs and spoons are also laid on the table.

'Janey!'

She returns to the bathroom to help Meg back onto her chair. Meg then gets herself into the kitchen and wheels herself to the table. Reaching for the muesli packet, she half-fills her bowl. It is important she eats healthily and keeps her weight under control as much as possible. No sugar anymore: now it's diabetic marmalade on the toast that, fortunately, Meg says is delicious, and blueberries on the cereal. Jane has a stash of Meg's favourite mint-and-choc-chip ice cream that she allows on high days and holidays.

Picking up the milk jug, Meg splashes some over her muesli. It slightly misses the mark and some of it goes onto the table. Jane, who hasn't yet sat down, pulls off a length of kitchen roll and passes it to Meg without a word, who blots up the spill wearing an exaggerated expression of tragedy but says nothing in response to Jane's dismissive wave. She takes the used piece of paper and chucks it in the kitchen swing bin.

The radio sits on the table and Meg switches it on – she's interested in current affairs and likes Radio Four when she's alone. Jane empties the kettle into the teapot, gives it a stir. She makes herself a mug of instant coffee then eats her own cereal. While Meg is still on her muesli, Jane leaps to her feet, kisses her on the cheek, apologises for her rush and reminds her Carys will be over at 10am. She unhooks her big padded jacket with the fur-edged hood from the rack in the hallway and puts it on. She is just about to leave the front door when Meg calls, 'Mobile, Janey.'

'Oh God! My fault, darling.'

Jane runs back to Meg's bedroom where her phone is on a charger beside her bed. Meg grins at Jane as she runs back into the kitchen and places the fully-charged phone carefully in an especially made elastic pouch attached to the outside of the chair. If Meg put it on her lap, she could drop it and it is vital she has it close to hand. Besides, her lap is the cat's place.

'Idiot!'

Jane turns back toward the door.

'Toast, Inspector.'

Jane turns back with comic timing. It's like a farce. She grabs the piece of toast from the toaster and drops it onto Meg's side plate. The spread and marmalade are nearby, spoons and knives already on the table.

'Sixes and sevens this morning. Left it a bit late.'

'Eights and nines at least.'

'I know. I just hate getting out of bed in this bitter weather.'

'Me too.'

Jane kisses the curly-haired top of Meg's head. 'Call if you need anything. Be good.'

'As though I could be anything else.'

Meg blows her a kiss. Jane glances back at her before she leaves the door. She is busy stroking Marmalade who has already settled on her lap.

Jane's Ford Focus Estate car splutters as she attempts to start it up and for a moment she thinks it may be going to refuse, but then it complies.

It starts as a fairly humdrum day at the Dyfed-Powys Police headquarters. A large building with a workforce of over a thousand full-time officers, the station covers the four counties of Pembrokeshire, Carmarthenshire, Ceredigion and Powys with a population of almost half a million people.

Today, a car is stuck in a snowdrift between Llangynin and

Castell Gorford and some of the men are drafted in to help clear the consequent pile-up of cars behind it.

A couple of shoplifters are caught on CCTV in Pembroke and need dealing with. A lad has to be stopped from climbing on the metal structure of a high bridge. A large dog bites a little one and the owner complains to the police.

But in a police station everything can quickly change, and at 2.07pm a missing person report comes in. On 2 January, a woman called Gwyneth who had been staying with her son in Swansea over Christmas and the New Year had been driven directly by him to a house she was cleaning in the afternoon near her home in the village of Moylegrove. The owners had promised to drive her home with her suitcase after she had 'done' for them. Apparently, she never appeared at this house, nor at her home and has not been seen since.

Her son, who claims he definitely left her outside the house where she cleans, is distraught. He called her on 3 January just to check she was okay but she hadn't answered her landline. Having tried a few more times, he'd then contacted her close friend and next-door neighbour who had been expecting to see her that day but there had been no sign of her. The neighbour who had a key to her friend's house has been in to look for her, but there are no signs Gwyneth has been in. No suitcase, no mail picked up from the doormat. No sign of her anywhere.

Late morning of 3 January the son files a missing person report with the Swansea police. But since the woman comes from the Dyfed-Powys Police area, it falls to that force to conduct the search. This is put into operation at once and it is all systems go.

Jane jumps into action and arranges for a forensic team to search the woman's empty home and a photographer to take photos. She has asked the woman's son from Swansea to meet her there where she and Detective Sergeant Ross Evans will interview him first and then the neighbour. Even though it is only about thirty-six miles it will take a good hour to drive there which means they won't reach Moylegrove till after 3.30. The time needed to do the interviews and see the lay of the land means Jane will be late back this evening. She calls Carys and Meg to let them know. Carys promises to stay late with Meg, who says there's some good telly on that evening so she'll be quite happy, and not to worry.

Jane organises some police officers to do house-to-house enquiries while others check hospital admissions and review CCTV footage in possible locations.

She buzzes Evans to her office to explain what they are about to do. A minute later, a thickset young man of distinctly rumpled appearance wearing a creased, mid-grey, ill-fitting suit, shoes that have seen better days and with slightly dishevelled spikey red hair knocks on her door. Answering her invitation to enter, he shuffles into her office in his characteristic way and stands awkwardly in front of her desk. This doesn't mean anything. Ross Evans may be an ungainly person but he's a good detective.

Jane gestures at the seat the other side of her desk. 'Afternoon, Evans.'

'Ma'am.' He sits on the tired wooden chair with the worn, red plastic seat.

'I'll explain in the car. We're off to Moylegrove, north Pem. A woman's gone missing. We have to leave now.'

'Missing? Sounds interesting. I'll just grab my recorder.'

In minutes with Evans at her side clutching his trusted recording equipment, they are on the road for the north where they will interview the woman's son and her neighbour. While they are up in Moylegrove, the Swansea police are conducting a covert search of the son's flat in case they find anything suspicious there.

It's annoying when there are two police forces involved on

the same job but it can't be helped in this case. They just have to co-ordinate their efforts to find the poor woman.

By 4.10pm, Jane and Evans have led cars with the rest of the people assigned to the job into the tiny, ancient village of Moylegrove. With a mix of traditional colour-washed and stone cottages and houses and a couple of stone chapels as well as a church and a quiet little river running through it, it is surprisingly unspoilt and turns out to be mostly Welsh-speaking. They find Gwyneth's house easily and meet the son there. A big, burly, overweight chap who looks as though he eats nothing but burgers shows them into his mother's immaculate small stone cottage with a garden at the back. Forensics go over it and Jane and Evans interview the son, Aled, and the neighbour and learn as much as they can discover about the missing woman.

Jane wants to see what the owner of the house where Gwyneth was supposed to have cleaned yesterday has to say. She gets directions from the helpful neighbour and with Evans at the wheel, driving – overcautiously as usual – they head up a bumpy grass track across farmland where sheep graze to a remote house a couple of hundred metres from the Pembrokeshire coastal path. Beyond this, steep cliffs drop down to what is at this time of year a fierce, dark sea.

They discover a fine renovation of an old, long stone house. The stone used is partly some of the original and partly a close match salvaged from derelict structures in the area. It even has its old oak door, darkened and weathered. The place is very beautiful. At least, Jane thinks so. Outsiders – mainly English people with money – are buying up old places like this one and saving them from collapse. She supposes this is the better way, but like most Welsh she holds a quiet grudge against those who buy and rent out property that might be used for the less well-off local people, instead of pushing up the cost of homes for holidaymakers who are only there part of the year.

'You do the honours, Ross Evans.'

When there is no one else around, she sometimes addresses him like this. Irritating though he can be, she's fonder of him than she will admit to herself. He lifts the heavy, old iron knocker and the door is soon opened by a tall, blonde woman who seems to be alone in the house.

Jane holds up her badge. 'I am Detective Chief Inspector Jane Owen and this is Detective Sergeant Ross Evans.' She gestures at Evans who nods his head.

'Hello,' replies the woman who is rather beautiful but white-faced with half-dead eyes.

'Good afternoon. May we come in, please? We just want to talk to you and ask you some questions with regard to a missing person, if that's all right?'

Reserved and polite she says, 'Yes, of course. Come in. But I am merely a guest here.'

'Oh, I see. And where is or are the owners?'

'I'm afraid the owner is out with his partner. They're hiking in Snowdonia at the moment. Maybe I can help?'

'Well, perhaps you can and since we're here now, if you don't mind, we'll come in.'

Jane steps through the porch and then another door into the expansive open-plan kitchen-living room. Her eyes scan the expensive interior. She and Evans are awed by the place. It must have cost a lot to convert. Jane puts out her hand to put the woman at her ease early on. A good technique that can be very useful with interviewees.

The woman is not antagonistic. She doesn't appear to be trying to hide anything. Although she comes across as surprised to see them she appears very willing to invite them in and tell them whatever they want to know. Jane says, 'Shall we sit at the table?' as she takes a seat on one side of the big oak dining table and removes a notepad and biro from her inside pocket. She motions to the woman to take the seat next to her, while Evans sits across from them.

'Right then. The purpose, aim and objective of our visit is to establish the whereabouts of a missing person and I should advise you that you can terminate this interview at any time.'

Jane takes the woman's details and fills her in about Gwyneth.

Evans helpfully summarises. 'So she was due to clean here yesterday afternoon on the 2nd January. But you say she never appeared? Can you tell us at what approximate time you called her landline?'

'Apparently, she was always punctual and very reliable, you know. Mike had left me her number so I called her... oh... at about 3.30, I'd say. It might have been a bit earlier. I was concerned as she was supposed to be here by 2.30. I tried again twice later with no luck. And this morning as well. I was very worried about her. Apparently, she's the salt of the earth, a lovely lady. I hope to goodness she's okay. Do you have any idea what may have happened to her?'

'Not at the moment.' Jane stood up. 'Well, that's all for now. Thank you for your help. If you hear anything, please let us know. And when the owners return, please ask them to get in touch. Here is my card. Thank you for your time.'

The woman ushers them politely to the door and later they check her phone records. The number she gave them had called Gwyneth's phone three times the previous afternoon and evening and twice early this morning.

They return to Llangunnor no nearer knowing what has happened to Gwyneth.

Land and air searches start early the following morning. Policemen along with search-and-rescue dogs and volunteers from the village, numbering about 200, all set out at 6.30am in the freezing conditions to search everywhere from wooded locations to open spaces. The air support unit hovers along the cliffs looking for any signs of a body over the side. They cover a large area but no luck comes of it.

The press and social media are alerted and there is an all-out hunt for Gwyneth from Moylegrove. A few reports of sighting come in but none lead to any result. The son was apparently the last person to see his mother. Having met the man, Jane harbours suspicions about him.

2

2014. CAMBRIDGE

In the spring of 2014, a dynamic, charming young woman called Bette Davies became bored of being alone. Named after the film star but pronounced Bet, she was looking for someone who was going places, with whom she could enjoy life, someone to benefit from knowing, someone from whom she could gain in knowledge and status. She scoured dating websites for men who lived in or near Cambridge. For some months she went on a large number of dates with men, all of whom had wanted to see her again, but none was up to the mark. Ambitious to find the right man, she was ready to look elsewhere.

Eventually in the autumn, she spotted a neat, stylish man who seemed in his photo to be good-looking with an air of being intelligent. She messaged him straight away and that evening received a reply that held much more interest than the usual uninspiring drivel men came out with, such as, 'I like nothing so much as cuddling up in front of a cosy fire with a lovely woman and a glass of red' or stuff about how they had a sense of humour – which generally meant they didn't.

But this Mike Hanson worked at a top firm of architects in Cambridge and said he loved creativity in others, blues and jazz and long country walks in solitary places. He said he cherished all forms of beauty from wonderful art and architecture to beautiful places and beautiful women.

He was, in other words an aesthetic man. If he liked beauty then he would like her. While not exactly vain, Bette was a realist who had every idea of her own good looks. So far, this Mike shaped up well.

They agreed on a time and a date, for which Bette wore her classiest knee-length blue dress and black stiletto shoes that set off her amazing long, shapely legs and slender figure.

Mike was instantly smitten but had done his best to disguise it as he didn't want to seem too keen too soon.

They had discovered they had much in common including a strong mutual attraction and a string of dates followed where Mike dined her at Cambridge's best restaurants, money appearing to be no object. One of these evenings, she mentioned she longed to get out of Cambridge and craved a walk in the countryside. He had been only too delighted to accommodate. He would collect her in his car the upcoming Sunday morning and whisk her out of the city to a remote rural spot.

Like all the men who had seen it, Mike had been struck by Bette's photograph online and she had more than lived up to the promise in the flesh. He had fast become fascinated by her and already felt he was falling in love. There was definitely something magnetic about her. Coupled with her high intelligence and great charm, she was a tall, sensual, sexy blonde with an erotic manner of moving. She dressed elegantly, which he liked in a woman; and when she had first bestowed her wide, delightful smile on him, he had been a goner. To him, everything about her – from her twenty-five years and her gorgeous looks to the way she spoke; from her likes and dislikes to the way she dressed; from her outgoing character to the fact that she liked doing the same things as he did – was just about perfect.

On an unusually cold November Sunday morning, Mike, a punctual person, drove his large, racy, blue BMW across Cambridge from where he lived just north of the river Cam to a side street of small Victorian terraced houses on the south side of the city centre.

He had been to Bette's flat in number 16 once before for a pre-dinner drink when he had tried planting the idea of buying a takeaway and spending the evening in since her flatmates were both out. But she had smelt his eagerness, spotted his hopeful strategy and rejected the idea on the grounds that one of the flat-mates might return and spoil their evening.

In other words, Bette was proving no easy nut to crack. She had been giving him mixed messages, flirting one minute, pulling back the next. This had challenged and stimulated Mike. In his opinion, too many girls were casually willing when it came to sex.

They had agreed 10am and, since he was not only a man of his word but a thoroughly careful one, he was precisely on time. It was impossible to find a parking space so he double-parked, rang Bette's mobile number, explained the difficulty and suggested she came out to the car.

An eager grin on her face, Bette came running out of her front door and jumped straight into the car. She was wearing an appropriate khaki-green puffer jacket and black leggings that showed off her legs that were tucked into stylish (and expensive) green wellington boots. He kissed her on the cheek and was rewarded with a wide flash of perfect teeth and a beautiful smile. She settled back in her seat.

He gazed at her, admiration in his eyes. 'You look gorgeous. But then you always do.'

'Hardly.' She laughed. 'I'm in my walking gear.'

'But still chic.'

Little did he realise she dressed almost exclusively in clothes bought on eBay or in second-hand shops.

'Glad you think so.' He really was a bit cheesy, she thought, but forgave him for his eagerness which was making him clumsy.

Having not seen his car before, Bette complimented him back, flattering his choice of colour which was, she said, as far as she was concerned, the best colour of that range of BMWs. He was glad she noticed.

'It has four-wheel drive.'

'Must be very handy in Cambridge.'

He made a face at her. 'I take it long distances and sometimes use it on dirt tracks or grass fields when I'm hiking. I've been far and wide in it.'

'Such as?'

'Oh – Cornwall – love the coastal path there; the Peak District, the Dales, the Lakes – anywhere with walking country where I get away from it all. It's my way of unwinding.'

'So where are we going today? Any of those places?'

'Not quite as far. But where is for me to know and you to wonder. Safety belt on?'

'What's with the mystery? Planning to lure me to some dark wood to have your wicked way with me?'

'Well, since you mention it...'

She wriggled in feigned excitement and he laughed. Things were hotting up in this relationship, sexual banter starting to replace their previously more formal exchanges.

They headed out of the city where they drove across flat, dull countryside towards Ely. Mike politely asked whether she minded if he played some music.

'Oh, please yes, most certainly, do.' For his sake, she pretended. He pushed a button on the swish dashboard and Billie

Holiday filled the car accompanying them as they drove through villages called Swaffham Bulbeck and Swaffham Prior where they turned left and drove into what appeared to Bette to be nowhere.

'My favourite singer of all time. I can never get enough Billie.'

For a moment Bette, who had never heard of her, was briefly perplexed by the name but soon worked it out. American. That's where women had men's names and she supposed men had women's though she couldn't think of an immediate example until she remembered Gene Kelly. But she nodded knowingly and said, 'Can't say I blame you.'

If he pursued the subject, she knew she was more than capable of bullshitting her way through questions about it. But for the moment he didn't, seeming satisfied that this beautiful young woman liked Billie too.

The horizon, distant and grey above perfectly straight lines of black land, was intercepted only by the occasional row of trees. Holiday's mournful lilt fitted with the desolate landscape that constantly repeated itself, canals and dykes taking the place of hedges separating vast, flat, gloomy areas that seemed too big to be called fields. Bette had never seen such a place in her life. Driving alongside them, they could never catch up with that horizon.

They finally arrived at a place called Wicken Fen. It was, he said, a good place to escape to. There were few other cars in the car park. It was cold and she was glad she had wrapped up well. He led the way to the start of their walk and her eyes followed the slightly lanky figure as he crossed the car park to a damp boardwalk that ran alongside a canal. She followed him and heeded his warning about the boards being slippery. When she got level with him, he placed a hand on her back and guided her in front of him onto the boardwalk. Once they were on it, he took the lead again. As they walked, Mike, who did seem to know a lot of things, explained that in the seventeenth century the fens that had stretched north of Cambridge into Lincolnshire had had channels and man-made canals dug across them to syphon the marsh waters off the boggy land.

'This is the only remaining original fenland that has been left undrained. A wondrous place.'

That he liked to demonstrate his knowledge from time to time had become apparent to Bette previously. Far from putting her off, she was a sponge who soaked everything in and enjoyed learning. He wasn't a show-off, though, and only mentioned little-known facts when he felt they were apposite or would interest her. Then he fell quiet and they picked their way along, happy to absorb the pleasure of silence, except once when he nudged her, put a finger to his lips and pointed to a heron fishing nearby. But the bird heard them and lifting its snake-like neck, pointed its head forward, slowly beat its wide wings and rose awkwardly from the murky wetland to flap low then slowly up towards a faraway tree branch.

They watched the bird life and the occasional ripple and splash where otters hunted, their breath converging with the nebulous mist floating over the water.

She liked being with this man who didn't feel the need to speak. She was making him happy by being there. Now certain this relationship was going the way she had hoped it would, she felt unusually peaceful. In no hurry, they wandered through the reedy, solitary landscape, embracing the calm environment. They reached an area of natural wetland where low grey water traced and fingered its way through wild grasses and a herd of stocky, dun-coloured ponies that grazed alongside russet Highland cattle. Standing quietly, they watched the animals in the ancient scene.

Mike turned to face her. She felt his intensity as he grasped her shoulders, pulled her to him and kissed her. He pushed his body against hers and carnal tension hung in the chilly air around them. Then he let go of her. 'You are a beautiful and fascinating woman and I long to know more about you. You've told me nothing about your childhood. Not even where you were brought up and I would love to hear all about your life up to now.'

They walked back toward the visitor centre.

'That's because I seldom talk about it. But I like you too.' Bette glanced at him to see his reaction. 'I'm sure you have already spotted traces of an accent?'

'Traces,' he said. 'There's a hint of Welsh, I'd say.'

'You're right, it's Welsh. So...' She took a large breath. 'I dislike talking about my past. But anyway, here goes. Me: well, me was an only kid brought up in a rural village in Pembrokeshire with an overly strict upbringing by old-fashioned, dyed-in-the-wool folk. That was me. We lived in a large house on a smallholding my father had inherited and where he continued to keep sheep as his pa had done before him. Disappointed I wasn't born a boy, he had little time for the female sex – which included Mother who worked all the hours, helping with the sheep as well as running the local village store. When I was very small, I recall being happier with her but as I grew this became lost along with her capacity for pleasure and her interest in me other than as someone to help with the chores.'

He interrupted. 'Whereabouts was this?'

'South Pembroke. Not far from Haverfordwest. Near a village called Hook where I was schooled.'

'I bet you got top marks in all your lessons.'

'Well, I didn't do badly but from the moment I learned to hold a pencil, I drew and painted patterns and designs and grew up absorbed by art and design. My parents never showed the slightest interest in my drawings nor encouraged me to do anything other than to help a great deal in the home and on the land. I was brought up hard and expected to work in the house and with the sheep from an early age. Truth is, my parents weren't that hard up at all. My dad had inherited quite a sum from his father. Anyway, when I wasn't cleaning floors or washing clothes, I was drawing, painting or burying my head in books. Whenever I could, I would take the bus to Haverfordwest where I would head for the library and order books on design and art. I also read novels, biographies, histories, travel books. Oh, I read and read. My parents scoffed at me for it but my English teacher used to bring books into school for me. She was really encouraging. Mr Jones, who taught art was too.' She stopped and walked on in silence.

'Hey, you can't stop there. It's an interesting story.'

'What else do you want to know?'

'More. Please expand.'

'Okay, so what can I tell you?' She stared at the ground. 'While they were watching TV in the evenings, about the only thing I can now bless them for is the learning I gained from reading so many books that I would never have done otherwise. I suppose I was self-educated to a degree. In the case of the interest in design and décor, inside the house was painted strictly magnolia throughout and my mother and father were set in their ways. My suggestions for new colour schemes for the rooms had been firmly resisted, but I had begged and begged my mother to let me paint my bedroom. When I was sixteen, she at last allowed it on the understanding that I must pay for the paint and the brush, and leave no mess.

'By that time I had left school and was working spare hours for my father helping with lambing, shearing in May or June and feeding forage to the sheep in winter. I also worked some hours in the bakery in Llangwm. When I had saved enough money, I caught a bus to Haverfordwest to buy the paint and brushes. I took them home and painted my room without

Mother or Father knowing. I wanted it to be a surprise. When I showed them the pale-pink bedroom I had always wanted, my mother said I'd put the mockers on the room and Father muttered, '*Ych-a-fi*,' and called me a *dimp*.

'A what and what?'

'Ooh, the first is a Welsh expression of disgust and a *dimp*'s a simpleton.'

'Harsh.'

'Then they insisted I repainted it. You can guess what colour. I have never quite forgiven them for that. Anyway, still determined to do that course in interior design in Cardiff, I became desperate to leave, I didn't tell my parents, who made it clear that they wouldn't consider funding such a ridiculous idea and wanted me to stay at home and continue working in the jobs I had... for the rest of my life. No thank you. I was so miserable and decided that if they wouldn't back me, I'd back myself. I worked really hard for a couple of years to save enough to pay for the course myself, in spite of having been expected to pay my rent from the day I left school.'

She stopped. But he persisted. '*And?*' he said, '*And?*'

'Oh all right then, but this is the bit that hurts. When I'd saved enough to cover my start-up expenses and the course, I left as soon as I could. I'd had enough of their controlling, over-strict, unkind parenting. I packed all I would need and took the coward's way, sneaking out one day while they were shopping in Haverfordwest. I wanted to take my beloved collie Brynn with me but knew I couldn't. Father was never kind to his dogs who worked so hard and gave him such devoted service. I used to sneak them treats behind his back and pet them when he wasn't looking. I remember the sun beating down that day – it was late August – but for me it felt like I was running through rain, I was so soaked in tears for leaving my dog. As for my parents, I haven't been in touch since and I doubt they've missed me for a second. I never felt loved by either of them.'

He draped an arm around her shoulders.

'One day I hope to get another–' Bette stopped herself. Whenever she thought about that dog it choked her and she was aware she had said enough. Besides, they had reached the car park and the blackened, weather-boarded café with its orange, pan-tiled roof. They went in and sat down at one of the small, round tables with two chairs.

'You're clearly a very brave person, Bette. You can't stop there. Please carry on.'

'I've really told you everything now.'

But he begged her to continue. Not wanting to come across as too secretive or reluctant to share her story with him, she steeled herself for the latter part.

'Well, I bussed it to Swansea where I caught a train to Cardiff. I'd already booked myself into a B&B and once there I soon managed to find a cheap bedsit to rent. Drab and small, it was nothing much to get excited about but a total joy to me. I could call it my own. I could breathe without criticism, drape scarves bought from charity shops over the ugly table and buy some bright cushions to cheer up the small sofa. At last I could eat, drink and do what I wanted. I was surprised by how bold I felt. The sense of freedom was incredible. I had already enrolled with the art and design college and started my course that September. At last I could express myself artistically and it seemed like the world had suddenly become my oyster.'

'It must have been fantastic for you.'

He gestured her to follow him up to the counter where an elderly woman asked what they would like. There was a big blackboard on the wall behind her and they chose sandwiches and a pot of tea for two. Told their order would be brought to them, they sat down at a small table. Mike leant forward. 'For such an incredibly attractive, sexy girl, there has to have been lots of men in your life. Tell me?'

She sighed and bowed her head. When she looked up, she flicked a long blonde lock out of her vivid blue eyes and observed him keenly.

'Okay. Last time I discuss it ever.' She paused and sighed. 'So, in Cardiff when I was twenty, I met a man, an art teacher, you know, who just took over my life. He was very attractive in a wild kind of way and lived on the edge. He would whisk me onto the back of his motorbike and drive dangerously fast while I clung on, wind stinging my eyes and the adrenaline of fear thrilling me. I admit he opened my eyes to just about everything from sex to surrealism. I fell madly in love, but what did I know?' She lowered her gaze to study the table. 'I moved in with him all too soon in what turned out to be a rubbish choice. David was a nasty man with a carefully masked sadistic bent who revelled in twisting my words and making me feel inferior. And to add some icing to that cake, within six months he was unfaithful as well, with one of my fellow students. I'll never forgive him for that.'

She didn't raise her head but lifted her eyes to fix a blue gaze on him. She watched his reaction. 'He was a total shit.' She looked quite miserable.

Unsure what to say, Mike mumbled, 'Oh no...'

'Please understand, Mike, that once I have told you this, I don't want to talk about it again. It upsets me to remember.'

'Give you my word.'

'About a year after we lived together, he was out on his Harley-Davidson one day when he was killed in a hit-and-run. In fact, if truth be told, once I got over the shock, it was actually a relief and I have to admit that I didn't really mourn for him. For a short while I continued to go it alone in Cardiff. I needed to be more self-sufficient so I learned to drive. Then, in pursuit of a complete change and to get away from such depressing memories, I drove south in an old banger I'd bought. I had read up about Cambridge and how it is one of the most desirable places to live in the UK, so I thought I'd try here. Once I made the move, I soon found a job assisting in an interior design shop while I lived in the grotty shared flat you've seen in the south of the city. As you know, I haven't made real friends with my three student flatmates, who are intent on partying and getting as drunk and high as often as possible. Not my sort of thing, besides I'm a bit older than them,' she murmured.

'You know what I'd really like now, Mr Hanson is as handsome does...' She stopped as though she'd forgotten what she was saying, 'is a great big *cwtch*.'

'So what's that, Ms Davies?'

'A Welsh hug. That's what I'd like.'

Mike stood up and walked round the table. 'Well, come on then, girl, stand up.'

And he gave her a big, long, warm *cwtch*. They stood like that for a while then their tea and sandwiches appeared on a tray in the hands of the amused older woman. 'How nice to see people so happy,' she said, beaming.

They sat down, smiled broad grins across the table and gazed at one another. She searched for her future in his eyes as he tried to see his in hers.

November 16th, 2014. Bette Davies' Five-Year Diary

Such a great day today. Best for ages. It might be that I'm falling. Mike is all right, that's for sure. Just about everything I could ever want. So handsome – can hardly tear my eyes away from his face. Lovely tall figure. Good hair. But clever too. Can be funny. V artistic and knows a lot. Could teach me so much. Best man I've ever found. Hope it works out. Really, really hope so. Fingers crossed. He seems v keen so it's looking good so far. Shall I sleep tonight? Doubt it.

3

5 JANUARY 2018. LLANGUNNOR, WALES

It is 10.08am when Sergeant Tom Griffith takes the 999 call. 'Dyfed-Powys Police headquarters, Carmarthen. May I help you?'

'I want to report a body,' says a voice.

'Right. Could I first ask you some details, please? Can we start with your name?'

'I am not prepared to reveal my name. I am just calling to inform you that there is a body in the sea in the Witches' Cauldron.'

'Okay, right.' The sergeant plays for time. 'Er, are you sure it's a body? Not a dolphin? Bottlenoses sometimes enter the cave, you know. Or, perhaps a dead seal?'

'It is a human body.'

'Right, okay, so can you tell me how and when you found the body then?'

'It is a human body.'

With no sense of urgency, Tom walks through the building to the DI's office and tells her what has just happened.

'So what did they say exactly?'

'That there's a body floating in the Witches' Cauldron. Up by Moylegrove,' he added.

'Caller's name?'

'They wouldn't give their name, ma'am.'

'Man or woman.'

'Woman, I think.'

'Trace the call, Griffith, and let us know, soon as.'

'Yes, ma'am.'

Jane calls the station at Fishguard, which is the nearest to the Cauldron. Fishguard has a skeleton coverage of two police community support officers. She speaks to the man on duty and asks if he can either get up there himself or get someone up to the place soon as to check the information given in the phone call is correct.

About fifty-five minutes later, she receives a mobile call from the shaken man confirming that it is indeed a body and that at this stage, he cannot be sure of the gender. Jane buzzes Evans.

'We have a body to recover, Evans. Possible homicide. Come in soon as, thank you.'

When he is sitting once again on the tired chair opposite her desk, Evans says, 'A body? Sounds interesting. Whereabouts?'

'Ceibwr Bay, the Witches' Cauldron of all places.'

'Sorry, ma'am, but I don't know it.'

'I went there years ago with my sister. It's on the Pembrokeshire north coast. Up where we were only last week. Near Moylegrove. Wild country up there as you'll recall. It's a massive, booming blowhole separated from the sea by this narrow bridge of rock. If you hit it at high tide the whole place is one great explosion of oceanic fury. It honestly has to be seen to be believed. Well-named actually. You literally have to climb over it to pass across it and if it's windy – which, my word, it can be up there – you're a brave or foolish person to go near it.'

Despite his scruffy appearance, Evans listens with great attention. 'So expect access problems, ma'am?'

Jane continues. 'It'll be choppy, so holding a boat still for a diver and photographer may not be so easy. If they go for overhead recovery, it'll need to be low tide to winch the body up. Have to send an abseiler down. It'll be treacherous enough whichever way it's done. Shame it's not summer time: the job would be a lot easier.'

'Put in a call to the coastguard then?' Evans suggests.

'We'll need to involve Fishguard coastguard to organise it. The police up there have only got one man on duty, and he's a support officer. Not much help, is it?' One hand holds the phone to her ear while the other cups the side of her brown-haired head. For some unconscious reason, it helps her concentrate.

'It's a technical job, retrieving a body full of gas and water from the sea,' says Evans. 'Best left to the experts. I'll put in a call to the underwater search team.'

Jane nods. 'Can you check the tides today, Evans. We'd better get a move on: it gets dark so early that there isn't much of a window for the rescue today. We might have to push a bit to get what we want.' She glances at her watch which reads just after 11am.

The DS scribbles on his notepad.

She tilts her head at him. 'Can you let me know what time it's happening, please? I'll want to be at the scene during the recovery. Thanks, sergeant. Catch you later.'

She checks the map on the wall behind her desk. She remembers the fantastic deep Cauldron from years ago when as a teenager she used to bring little Meg along to walk the coastal path on summer weekends. She remembers Meg picking wild flowers to take home to Mam and how they had heard about the hidden cave accessible only by sea tunnels – apparently a sea-witch's lair – that once you entered you never left.

She remembers them finding it and the overwhelming, unique and beautiful scenery. Lost for words, they had walked over the narrow rock arch and looked down at the brilliant green water below. But that had been summer time and the sea had been calm with kayakers paddling around the cavernous waters. For a moment she feels intensely sad. But there is no time for that.

They'll need a police Land Rover as the narrow roads are treacherous at the best of times.

She decides they should drive as near as they can but that they mustn't take risks. She plots a place to stop the police cars, from which they can walk to the cave. They'll need walking boots, trekking poles and ropes to secure themselves against falling but they have that gear at the station. The police in West Wales quite often have need of them.

She calls Evans in and tells him to tell the officers to have the cars, boots, poles et cetera at the ready. He nods and leaves the office, closing the door behind him. A few seconds later, he knocks, opens it again and pops his ginger head around it. 'Sorry, Inspector, but what size feet do you have?'

She is standing studying the map. She turns. 'Bit personal, Evans.' She cocks an eyebrow, tips her head to one side and gives him a wry smile. 'But if you insist, I'm a four, as it happens.'

He grins and nods a thank you. As he leaves, he thinks what fun the inspector can be at times while at others she can be really tetchy. But then her plate is overflowing, the poor love. Inwardly, Evans feels protective towards his gritty little boss and always tries his best for her.

Itching to get there, Jane decides that if they cannot arrange a coastguard today, she'll drive up there anyway. When a body is found floating in water, it doesn't immediately mean an accidental drowning. She thinks about movies where bodies are dumped into rivers and shipping lanes. If a person drowns, it could mean suicide, it could mean accident or, God forbid, it could mean murder.

It will usually take quite a few days for the body to return to the surface of the water. Gut bacteria stay alive after the body has died. They continue to make carbon dioxide that eventually fills the body with gas, causing it to float. She supposes the body must have been there for some time.

The pathologist will give them a clearer idea once they've retrieved the body. The news comes in that the tide is at its lowest at 1746 today. Once that happens a small pebbly beach will appear in the cave for the abseiler to stand on. Jane takes the decision to go before darkness but as late as possible. The abseiler will be able to stand in shallow water. She checks to find that sunset is at 1623. She asks if the coastguard can help at 1545 and is assured that they are on standby with a rope access specialist at the ready. A lifeboatman has been commandeered to take a small motorboat with a police photographer into the cave at the same time. It's a rough sea so it won't be easy for the men in the boat. They have been told to help the coastguard get the body onto a stretcher that will be lowered from above. They are experienced chaps in the coastguard and they will know to choose the safest possible place to descend from.

DS Ross Evans drives Jane in a police Land Rover, a couple of officers following in a van in which to transport the body to the morgue. It takes about an hour to drive north to Moylegrove. The land is still covered with the remains of the snow that has partly melted then refrozen. It is not far from the Cauldron, about twenty minutes on foot. But Jane has mapped the route and with Sergeant Evans feeling slightly nervous, they drive on along a narrow lane towards the coast. They find a spot where they can park on the edge of the lane and walk the rest of the way. They have walking poles, necessary in these conditions when you get close to the edges of the cliffs, some of which are crumbling in places. It is about one degree above zero with a chill that in spite of their thick puffer jackets, they can feel cutting through them. Their faces hurt from the bite of the wind.

∾

By half past three that afternoon, Jane and Evans are standing on the frost-covered south side of the Cauldron as near to the cliff edge as they dare.

'How deep would you say it is, ma'am?'

'I'd guess about 200 feet.'

'Agree, ma'am. I'd say so too.'

Jane glances at Evans who is paler than usual. But for once he is not shuffling. *Shows he doesn't have to,* she thinks.

A couple of coastguards, two officers from Fishguard and an extra trained climber to aid the descent are already waiting. Jane peers down, scanning the choppy water. It is not easy to see at first but she eventually spots the corpse in a corner emerging from some overhanging rock. A disturbing sight, it seems something has hold of its feet as the waves buffet it about. A life-size balloon figure in a dark coat bobbing about in the water. Jane fiddles to get a clear focus through her binoculars. She moves the glasses to the swollen, bloated mess of a face but it is too far to get a proper look.

They wait for the tide to go out a little further and as edges of the beach begin to appear the climber starts to descend the sheer, ragged edges of the blowhole. Slowly, he moves across the rock face toward the patch of large pebbles.

At approximately the same time, a small motorboat slowly enters the cave through a tunnel of rock. It is battered and rocked by the sea but its highly experienced skipper is a lifeboat crew member. He sees the body and drives the boat as close and as steady as he can in the choppy, tricky waters while the photographer leans forward, studies the body and shoots some pictures.

The diver lowers himself carefully over the side of the boat into the sea and swims to the body's feet. Watching through her binoculars, Jane sees that what has hold of the body is not a witch but a fissure into which, thrown by the waves at the rock face, one foot has become wedged. The diver sets about releasing the trapped foot while the climber descends to the small beach. Having freed the body, the diver drags it through the water to the climber. Jane bets they feel queasy as, from what she can now see, the body is not a pretty sight.

A stretcher has been lowered down after the climber. The diver helps and the two men cover, strap and secure the distended, heavy corpse to it.

The coastguard officer above gets the thumbs up and slowly winches the body upwards while the climber goes up alongside it, helping to keep it level to prevent it from hitting the rockface.

Everyone claps when the man makes it back to safety. He shudders with relief. It is definitely the worst thing he has ever had to do. The horrible remains of a face, mouth minus lips gaping, the swollen body blued by the water with its enormous pregnant-looking belly almost bursting out of its coat, puffed up thighs and cracked, wrinkled walking boots is a shocking sight. It looks barely human. Even the fleece gloves have been nibbled at. Safely covered, the stretcher must now be carried by two men on foot across the steep, slippery, dangerous terrain. It's quite a way back to the van and they must be as quick as they can. When a submerged body that has been in cold water is brought ashore, decomposition will happen at an accelerated rate. Even after just a few hours, its appearance may be completely changed; so it should be examined as soon as possible.

Standing watching the scene, Jane hears one constable say to the other, 'As kids we were scared of the place and would never go near the edge. Good thing we didn't. The witches down there are real, it seems.'

Jane and Evans return to Fishguard where they grab some sandwiches and tea. While she eats hers in her makeshift office, the police photographer arrives with a clutch of printed photos of the body in the water. Jane pins them to the temporary whiteboard that has been hastily erected on one wall of their new room. She writes down the details of the case as known so far.

Now she calls Carys, who never delays answering. She is as reliable as anyone can be although quite often she does nip back to her own house with various excuses when she should really stay with Meg. But Jane knows she was lucky to find her and that she is a good woman with a kind heart.

'Carys, sorry to call again so soon, but I'm going to be late back. Not sure what time. We've had a major incident here and it's going to take up a lot of my time. I'm going to need your help even more than I usually do.'

Carys interrupts, 'No worries, no worries at all. Now then, Jane, all you got to do is just tell me what's needed, see, and then you know you can leave it to me, if you know what I mean.'

'Oh Carys, you're my saviour. A real angel. For tonight I'll need you to go in at about six thirty and get Meg her tea. Then would it be okay to stay with her till I get back? Should be at about eight-ish.'

'I'll just have to pop back to get my husband his tea after but apart from that I'll stay with Meg. No worries, no worries,' says Carys again. 'I'll go across now, in a minute.' Jane knew well what that phrase meant but also that Carys would not let her down. Carys' husband Tom works as a carpet-fitter in Carmarthen.

'Oh, thank you. And could you please feed Marmy?'

'Of course I will, Janey, of course I will. You know you can trust me. You can trust me.'

'Carys, I know I can do that.' Carys does so love to fish for approbation. 'Can I call you in the morning and fill you in a bit more – so sorry but in a bit of a rush right now. Bless you. Speak tomorrow.'

'No worries, no worries,' she can hear Carys saying as she rings off. As she leaves the police station, she thinks it's funny the way the woman invariably repeats herself. Then, taking Evans with her, she drives to the coroner's office in Milford Haven to see the forensic pathologist assigned to the case.

A tall, greying, avuncular man, Max Granger is bent over a naked, swollen, green-and-purple female cadaver lying face up in a shallow metal bath. He dictates to his eager young female assistant as he examines the body. She has a recorder switched on in case she misses anything. In a matter-of-fact tone, he articulates his observations.

'Well, let's see. Female, hard to tell the age on account of water damage to the skin but twenties to thirties, certainly not older. Maceration of the skin, pale areas of hypostasis, adipocere formation and where the skin has absorbed the water it has begun to peel away from the underlying tissue...'

One cheek has a flap of wrinkled flesh extending outward from the face. It has clearly been gnawed at but then most of the rest of the facial flesh is missing. The flesh around the mouth is completely missing and the exposed teeth grin in a grotesque manner. Both eyes are also gone. The entire corpse is disgustingly white and wrinkled. Even through their masks, the stench can be easily detected. But Max doesn't notice. He is so used to the smell of formaldehyde and decaying flesh. He studies one of the corpse's thighs where something has managed to get in through the clothing and has nibbled a fair amount of flesh. It's astounding how quickly these sea creatures cotton onto a free meal.

'Give us a hand, would you?' He nods to his assistant who helps him roll the body over, which must be done with great care.

Among many other contusions where the body has smacked against rock, Max spots a small, livid, circular bruise in the lower centre of the back. Holding a magnifying glass over it, he studies it for some time before measuring it with a minutely precise tool while declaring the figures out loud.

Having finished with his exam of the outside of the corpse, he now indicates he needs help to roll the body over onto its back again. The girl obliges.

Max fetches a large, intensely-sharp knife and slowly splits open the trunk of the body, starting at the gullet and cutting carefully right down the centre to the groin. He peels back the flesh as he goes. He then cuts through both sides of the rib cage, before cutting out the sternum with two sides of ribs still attached to it. He puts the whole thing to one side. Now the lungs, heart and trachea become visible. Thick, sticky blood has pooled either side in the chest cavities. This he ladles into a plastic jug and tips down the drain at the bottom of the bath. Having disposed of two jugs-full, he then removes the high internal organs. Putting them on a table to one side, here with a smaller knife he first slices open and examines the trachea followed by the lungs and then the heart.

With the same knife he now removes the face and hair all in one piece, leaving a bald, faceless scalp and head. Taking a hacksaw, he saws away across the front of the head to get at and remove the brain, which joins the other body parts on the table.

Apart from the noise of the saw on bone, silence has reigned while he has been at this gruesome work but now, he speaks again. His assistant switches into high alert.

'I am fairly certain death took place in the water and that the victim was conscious when she went in. A slightly bloody froth cone is present in the airway where mucous, air and water have mixed during respirations. This indicates she was alive when she went in. There's bleeding into the sinuses, which have several millilitres of water aspiration and debris from the water has accumulated in the lungs.'

Working fast with frowning concentration, Max injects the sternum with a thin needle and withdraws some bone marrow into a syringe which he carefully carries across the room to an area where there is an array of microscopes. He gently depresses the plunger until a drop of marrow plops into a petri dish, which he places under one of the microscopes. His tense young assistant follows, anxious not to miss a thing.

'Yes,' mutters Max, 'as I thought. Traces of diatoms in the bone marrow indicating the heart was beating at the time she went in.'

It is getting on for seven o'clock in the evening when, before going into the examination room, Jane and Evans are given white masks to wear over their mouths and noses.

Max crosses over to the corpse just as Jane and Evans come into the lab. Evans takes one look at the body and starts to quietly heave so Jane points him to the door. He leaves as fast as he can.

'Mr Granger, thank you for seeing us so late in the day. I'm afraid my detective is faint-hearted and I thought rather than have him throw up in here, it would be better if he left. Have you reached any conclusions so far?'

'Oh, don't worry about the poor chap. He won't be the first and he certainly won't be the last. And call me Max, will you? You are?'

'Jane,' she answers this kind man who looks to be in his late fifties. The committed type, she would say. He shakes her hand. Appreciative of this highly experienced man for making her not feel young and green, Jane eagerly returns the handshake. He is treating her as an equal and so many of his age do not.

'Well Jane, here is what I know so far. Decomposition has started and the outer skin layer has loosened, what we call "washerwoman syndrome". So I would say she's been dead about a week. We'll never know precisely.' He points out parts of the corpse to which he refers as he speaks. Jane, watching him closely, notices he is good-looking.

'There is no evidence that I can find so far of any natural disease. There are multiple contusions, cuts and abrasions from when the body fell or from where it got smashed against the rocks by the tides. From the lividity and scrapes on the corpse, I think it lay on its back on the seabed for a time. Crabs and such-like have made quite a feast of the face. Only bare bit of body exposed, so that's not unexpected.'

He beckons his assistant to help roll the cadaver over. 'Interestingly, I have been able to distinguish one small, round, livid bruise in the middle of the victim's back which happened about the time she went into the water. It may well have been caused by whatever pushed her off the edge. It is clear it was also used on the coat she was wearing, which, by the way, has blood spatters on the fabric, not the victim's, but of someone other.'

Together with his assistant, he then rolls the body onto its back again. 'We'll see if we can match the DNA and the dental records, of course.'

Max says the bruise puzzles him. Tomorrow, he assures Jane,

he will send over the photos by email and hopes to have drawn some conclusion as to what might have caused it.

Unexpectedly, Jane's mind now sees and smells another body. A terribly burnt one. She only knows it is her father by the wedding ring. To begin with after this happened, sleep gave up on her. At night, she would struggle with repeated recurring images. At the time the PTSD counselling, kindly provided free by the force, helped somewhat; but even now these flashes still occasionally happen. Rubbing her forehead to rid it of the image, she forces herself to concentrate on the here and now.

'Anyway, as I was saying, I'm sorry I can't be more use. You see, the cooling rate of victims of drowning depends on water temperature and movement. The cave experiences a lot of rapid water movement and this would slow down the cooling. On average, a body in cold water will cool twice as fast as a body on land. Rapid skin cooling may cause a person to inhale water or suffer sudden cardiovascular collapse and drown even though he or she might be a good swimmer. But in that place in these temperatures, there was no chance. The icy cold would have done the job. I suspect death would have been in a matter of minutes. Not more. But on account of that bruise, it is looking like murder.'

'Murder, no less.' Jane's heart flutters. It will be on her shoulders.

'By the way, there are still a number of tests that remain to be done, including the stomach contents. I hope to finish most of them by tomorrow.'

Jane glances at her phone. The time is quarter to eight. She could be home by half past eight if she gets a move on. She realises she's starving hungry.

'I'd better get on. Thank you so much for everything.' The name Max sticks in her mouth as her training tells her to call him 'sir'. She thinks it's because he is much older than her. She stumbles over her words, 'Mr Gra... I mean Max,' then giggles like a schoolgirl. Immediately feeling foolish for behaving so stupidly, she realises it is because there's something very attractive about this intelligent, dedicated man who is tall and handsome. But Max, whose head is buried in close examination of the liver, is so committed to his work he hasn't noticed her silliness.

'Good to meet you, Jane. Bye-ee.'

'Bye, now. We'll speak tomorrow and I may see you again then.' *Thank God,* she thinks. She has got away with it. *Wait till I tell Meg – me, a DCI giggling in front of that dreadful body – perhaps it was because of that. It certainly was a gruelling experience, especially having that awful flashback.* She had to remain steady – it was her job, more so since Evans had been such a wimp. She might have known he would be.

Evans collects the victim's clothes, boots, a ring and a corroded, dark-coloured chain necklace with a small cross on it. He brings the bagged evidence to the station. He says he's starving too. Poor Ross lives in Carmarthen so he'll get back even later than Jane.

On the way home Jane takes pity and lets him stop at a garage shop and run in to grab some crisps, a choc bar and a drink to keep him going. He gets her a bag of crisps too.

She tells herself that tomorrow she must arrange a thorough search of the ground surrounding the Cauldron. She also makes a note to check the weather conditions from a week ago. That it snowed over the whole of Pembrokeshire soon after Christmas she remembered clearly so it must be taken into account for covering tracks and evidence.

Murder. Her mind buzzes with a mix of excitement and anxiety. She loves the idea of the chase and the thrill of catching a guilty person. She enjoys the thought of finding them, but more, the interviews that follow. She will prepare well for those interrogations and will sit with the suspect as long as it takes.

When confronting the most disturbing individuals, whether they're arrogant, cunning or manipulative or, as they often are, all three, she will use these traits against them. She knows they will come into the room already judging her and certain they're smarter than her so she will make sure to appear gullible to them. She will play dumb while they talk and talk and as late as possible in the game strategically reveal what she knows. But before this can happen, she needs to find the killer.

4

NEW YEAR'S EVE, 2014. CAMBRIDGE

They were celebrating the end of the year at a dinner in a Cambridge restaurant near Magdalene Bridge. The more Mike saw Bette, the harder he fell and more love-struck he became. For a reason he couldn't explain, he had felt an instant kinship with her. Normally a pragmatic man and certainly no fatalist, with this woman he had felt as though their destinies were linked.

He had done well at university where he had read architecture and shown a flair for it. Cambridge had become his new home and the only place he felt centred and so he had applied for jobs there. He could perhaps have chosen to go to London where there would have been greater opportunities for a young architect of his calibre but he had grown to love the city he was in. Where else would you be surrounded by such awe-inspiring buildings as the old colleges? So when he had been offered a job with the foremost firm of architects, he had snapped it up.

Mike's keen eye for beauty influenced to whom he was sexually attracted. Unconsciously, he modelled women on his mother, a tall, attractive, long-haired woman who had given him strong guidance through his childhood. In every sense she had shown strength except when it had come to her deeply unfaithful and unkind husband, to whom she had never stood up. Perhaps also Mike's boyhood crush on Madonna had forever influenced the appeal certain types of females had for him. Although the singer had quite often changed the colour of her hair, his abiding image of her was a gorgeous blonde seductress wearing highly revealing clothes. The dominatrix thing had had him writhing in his teenage wet dreams and he still quietly fantasised about women in stilettos cracking whips over him. But he kept those fantasies well-hidden as he was a shy man who would never allow them to surface. When he had been in his first year at university and had visited Paris with a couple of male undergraduate friends, he had never quite recovered from his first visit to the Quartier Pigalle, the infamous red-light district where a beautiful, long-haired blonde had given him the happy ending massage to end all happy endings.

Apart from Bette's gorgeous, wavy, long blonde hair which he loved, as well as what he considered to be a perfect figure, he could not stop looking at her pretty, pixie-like face with its wide blue eyes, pert nose and firm chin. But perhaps the most attractive thing about her was the strength of purpose she so clearly tried to hide. She also had a big sense of humour and could make him laugh – most women didn't – and that he much appreciated.

Her strong artistic streak and love of walking in remote areas fitted in so well with his pastimes which veered between visiting art galleries and hiking long distances. Her enjoyment of books, her high intelligence and, apart from what must have been a Welsh need for rice and chips together, she ticked all the boxes.

He might have expected her to be needy because of her bad childhood – but she was not. She was a straight-talker and a down-to-earth sort of girl. All in all, as far as he was concerned, she was as near perfect as it was possible to be.

When it came to questions about her parents, Bette refused to talk about them as people. Believing she had good reasons – because she was a person who did nothing without them – Mike left the subject alone. Being something of a closed shop himself, he understood completely and knew too well that there are certain things you never wish to discuss with anyone. It seemed that when she had left home, she had become remarkably self-sufficient. He accepted her eagerness to hide her roots as a simple desire to better herself but he did enjoy her occasional slip back into Welsh expressions that she couldn't quite get rid of like 'there's lovely' and 'I'm only saying'.

Although not in detail, she had told him about her bad experience with what she called a 'total washout' marriage and this evening she expected him to tell her about his past. He tipped his chair back and fiddled with the piece of bread on his plate before saying, 'Much as I'd rather not discuss it, it has to be done. It needs exorcising.'

He took a large glug of wine. Finding this far from easy, he told her about his parents. How his British father had made millions in property and bonked almost as many women. How his poor, long-suffering mother, Australian by birth and whom he took after, had forgiven her husband time and time again. His father had died of a heart attack in 2007 and Mike had inherited what he described cautiously as 'a decent sum', though it hadn't made up for his lack of fathering and his appalling behaviour toward Mike's beloved mother.

What had really hurt was when his mother had decided to return to her homeland while he was still at university.

'Oh yes, I was self-sufficient.' He steepled his fingers before clasping his hands together and frowning, staring at the tablecloth. 'I mean, I had money that bought me a house and car etc, but I still needed support and love, didn't I? I was only nineteen years old. I try to get over there once a year, usually for

45

Christmas and she comes over every three years or so, but I cannot ever quite forgive her for betraying me by going back to Australia. I mean, it's just so far. Besides, since she remarried, it's not the same...' His voice trailed off but the bitterness was in his tone and Bette saw how hurt he had been by his beloved mother's leaving. To call it a betrayal was pretty strong, but it was indicative of how alone he had felt when she had gone.

'I'm sorry, Mike. You have clearly been very hurt. And what about *your* love life?'

He hesitated. 'My last year at uni, I fell for a woman. She went out with me, slept with me, seemed to make me happy and after a year, just as I was preparing to ask her to marry me, she suddenly, with no apparent reason, ditched me. She simply disappeared from my life. She blocked my calls, refused to respond to messages, wouldn't answer her doorbell when I rang it.' He sighed heavily. 'Whatever I tried I could not get her to speak to me again. I have to admit I even stalked her for a short time. I know that's terrible, but I was so confused by her behaviour that I just wanted to catch up with her and speak to her. Surely, I thought, there must have been a reason she had so rapidly gone off me. I went from hero to zero overnight with no explanation. She had given me every reason to be sure she loved me. That was what was so very strange.' He looked uncomfortable talking about it but Bette wanted to know and encouraged him to finish his tale.

'Well, it took me ages to recover from this. I suppose I was what they call broken-hearted. Afterwards, I suffered from grave self-doubt and found it so difficult to get my life back on track. I developed big issues with trusting women and in the end simply stayed away from them and instead buried myself in my career.

'Then, I decided enough was enough and that I needed to get a grip. I longed to meet someone to fall in love with but doubted it would ever happen. Until recently. This autumn my life changed when I met someone. A woman I fancied to bits, adored her mind, in fact, as far as I was concerned, she was almost perfect...' He paused and grinned. 'But thank God not altogether or she would have been boring. Something that, I hasten to add, is the last thing she could ever be.'

He raised his glass to her and said, 'Might there be a chance that feeling could be reciprocated?'

'There might be,' she said but avoided looking at him.

He wondered if he'd said too much too soon. After all, she'd had a bad experience with a man before.

They drank champagne, had smoked salmon starters, then he had a fillet steak and French chips while she had duck with cherry sauce and gratin potatoes. They had an especially good French wine. Offered the dessert menu, he said, 'I'm not a lover of sweet things so I'll have the cheeseboard, please.'

Bette raised the natural arch of her eyebrows. 'Maybe I could change your mind, Mike Hanson?'

'Coquettish, aren't you? As to your question, you are, of course, the exception that proves the rule.' They finished eating and he ordered Irish coffees, since she said she had never experienced them before.

Around them, irritated wives and girlfriends thought, *What more stereotypical look-at-me kind of girl could there possibly be?* The men eating with them were unable to stop themselves ogling the blonde in the long-sleeved, tight-fitting, low-cut red dress that showed off her intensely alluring figure. Mike too, could not take his eyes from her and aware of the attention she was getting, felt a mix of intense jealousy and immense pride that she was with him.

They were on the way to being drunk by the time the waiter brought the trolley on which was a flambé burner. With a camp flourish and practised finesse, he heated the whisky, coffee, sugar and other ingredients on the burner before pouring the thick, dark liquid into the glasses where it gleamed as he slowly poured snowy white cream over the back of a teaspoon to float on top.

Halfway through drinking them, Mike stood up and leant forward, looked her in the eyes and taking his napkin to her lips, shouted with laughter. The rest of the diners stopped what they were doing to watch. Another side of Mike revealed itself.

'Bette Davies,' he said so they all could hear, 'you've got cream all round your mouth.' With a flamboyant gesture he wiped it away. 'This is so that I can kiss you without getting covered in the stuff.' Placing his arms on either side of the table as he almost knocked everything over, he leant across. 'Come here,' he said. She stood to his command. He kissed her hard on the lips and in between kisses, said, 'I want you' *kiss* 'to come and' *kiss* 'move in with me' *kiss* 'as soon as' *kiss* 'possible.' Then he sat down and leant back in his chair.

'Well?' he said

She also sat down and tossed her blonde mane back from her face. In proper broad Welsh, with that brilliant smile on her face, she said, 'But we only met three months ago.' The diners watched with bated breath. Then, slipping back into something close to received pronunciation, she said, 'So you may be surprised to learn, Mr Michael Hanson, that the answer is "I'm going to think about it tonight and let you know in the morning."' She gave a dramatic pause. 'But just so's you knows, I'm woman overboard, me, and one thing's for sure and that is that I loves you loads and loads.'

And everybody clapped including the waiters and the manager. And they stood up and the two of them took a bow.

Mike paid the bill and she went to the ladies'. He laughed when she had reappeared wearing a pair of fur-lined ankle boots and carrying her red stilettos in a string bag. But he liked and approved of her forethought and when he had helped her on with her long red scarf and warm, caramel-coloured, cashmere coat with the fur collar, she looked as elegant as she had in the red dress.

They walked through the cold streets to Midsummer Common which was packed with people revelling. Turned up to full volume through the large speakers that had been set up for the occasion, Big Ben striking midnight sounded out across Cambridge. Before they kissed again, Bette and Mike leant into one another, looked at one another and said simultaneously, 'Happy New Year.'

Mike lived in a beautiful four-bedroom Victorian house in a quiet, traffic-free street just north of the Cam and Midsummer Common. It appealed to Bette in every way. Mike was gratified when she said, 'It's such a surprise inside. You've done a great job on it. I completely love it.' It was indeed very much to her taste.

The long living room had originally been two small rooms. Mike had painted the walls dark blue and hung up a few modern paintings and complemented them with white doors, floors, skirtings and fireplace. He had a few bits of Danish modern furniture and white rugs on a pale, painted wooden floor. White pendant lights in unusual shapes finished the room with what Bette decided was inspired flair and so different from most middle-class interiors. The kitchen was modern but done in soft Mediterranean colours and exposed old brickwork. It had large French doors that looked onto a lovely garden. She supposed the place was in keeping with a modern architect's mind.

Once before, they had attempted to grab some hurried sex at the flat Bette shared with two girls who had both been out that evening, but just as they were ready to bare all to one another, a flatmate had unexpectedly returned in floods of tears following a row with her boyfriend.

Mike had delayed suggesting she spent the night with him for fear of frightening her off. But that evening had changed everything. They were in love and wanted to be together. Just to be sure, Mike wanted to know that Bette felt the same way the following morning. He knew he would, of that he was certain. They were both full enough of alcohol to lower any inhibitions and didn't waste any time, literally running up the stairs to Mike's bedroom where he hurriedly stripped her before lifting her up and laying her on the bed. A passionate night of sexual exploration and mutual gratification followed. In the morning, they made love for the fourth time before collapsing in exhaustion where they lay in one another's arms until 11.30am when Mike brought a tray of hot coffee, warm croissants and marmalade. They ate and drank sitting up in bed, flakes of pastry falling from their lips and fingers. Bette, who missed little, had already learnt he was a fastidious man and noticed him carefully picking up each fallen flake and dropping them on the plate.

The following weeks before she moved in, they made love as often as possible. She moved some of her stuff to his house while holding onto her room in Gwydir Street that, without the landlord's knowledge, she sublet for three months for a little bit more than she had been paying. So she was, as they say, quids in.

Mike had happily encouraged her not to burn any bridges back to where she had been before meeting him. While he would describe himself as careful (he always looked neat and clean with manicured fingernails) 'impulsive' was the word he'd have chosen for Bette.

Had he known what lay ahead, he might have picked another word.

5

6 JANUARY 2018, 06.02AM. LLANGUNNOR, WALES

Jane wakes early after a nightmare in which her sister's screaming face featured. She rubs her eyes and peers at her bedside clock. It is only just after six o'clock. The dream had been close to what had actually happened except that for some reason their grandmother's face suddenly appeared in the train, asking Meg for a slice of cake. Jane's anger with such an absurd request when the woman could surely see she needed help to get Meg out of the carriage was intense and she started yelling at her long dead mamgu. That is when she has woken and she finds it hard to rid her head of the image of her screaming sister lying in agony, trapped. She rolls over and tries to put it from her mind.

She doesn't need to leave for the station until 7am. Carys is coming over to help Meg get dressed later and get her breakfast ready at nine. Nice for Meg to have a lie-in, which she loves. Jane drags herself up at 6.20, has a hurried wash, dresses, grabs a bowl of cereal and a coffee, calls the cat in, feeds him and tiptoes out. The cold hurts her face in the tiny distance between the front door and her car and she is so glad the car decides to start.

She has to drive slowly in the dreadful conditions but she is at her desk early today. There's much to be done.

Almost as soon as she gets to the station, Jane receives a call from Max.

'I may be onto something. Regarding the contusion on the victim's back, it is clear that something hard and sharp prodded it. A hunch led me to bring one of my own trekking poles into the exam room. I compared the tip with the mark on the body and the back of the puffer jacket. It's an exact fit. I have a feeling one of these was used to nudge the poor woman forward over the cliff edge. I'm sending some photos now. Bad news is, no DNA match to be found. No dental records either. Unusual, but the woman had damn near perfect teeth – not a filling to be seen – and had no evident dental work done that I could see, which may explain the lack of luck there.'

'Oh no. That's not exactly helpful at all.'

'It is not. By the way, our boys have taken soil samples of the land around the top of the hole. They are being analysed now. I'm looking at stomach contents this morning.'

Jane's own heaves at the thought. 'Right.'

'Let you know later if there's anything suspicious to add.'

'Thank you, Max. Look forward to hearing from you later and to seeing the photos.'

Intently, Jane watches her computer's mailbox and within a minute, the photos arrive as an attachment to a short note from Max. She prints them out, collects them from the printer drawer and takes them with her to the incident room where she winds her way through the desks. At the end of the room, she secures the photos to the whiteboard. Then she faces the room and clears her throat. They all stop what they're doing and look up at her. There are some cynical older faces out there, which might daunt her if she allowed it to, but she doesn't.

'Right. I want everyone's full attention, please.'

They're on their mettle and bristling with interest. Jane moves to the blown-up map of Pembrokeshire that she earlier readied on the board. She stands next it, pointer in hand.

'Right.' She points first to the site on the map, then to a photo of the Cauldron which is now surrounded by incident tape. 'Most of you will have been up to the Witches' Cauldron at some time, but for those who haven't, I suggest you get yourselves up there for a gander soon as you can. It's important to get a feel for the place.' She pauses. They are rapt. 'So far, we have female victim unknown, age around mid-twenties to mid-thirties. Hair blonde. Cause of death drowning, motive unknown but we will definitely be treating this as murder. The DNA had no match. Dental records are still being traced, but no luck so far.'

The police officers shuffle in their seats. She points to a photograph of the bruise on the back of the body and then to an image of the puffer coat removed from the corpse. 'We're still looking for the trekking pole that caused this bruise. And still no reports of a missing woman fitting the description, local or otherwise.'

The officers take surreptitious glances at one another. Jane points at the photo of the ravaged face. 'I know it's a tall order but it is essential that we find out who this is.' They follow her lead. She may be young but she runs a tighter ship than her predecessor and they know it. Standing by the board, pointer in hand, she indicates a photo of the repulsive blown-up body.

'All right. So, so far, we have victim unknown, motive unknown but it is definitely looking like murder. There was a local missing Moylegrove woman reported two days ago, so far untraced, but she is in her late fifties and does not correspond to the description of our Jane Doe. It's still a hell of a coincidence, though, and must be borne in mind. You probably know about it but I want you all to study these posters of her as a missing person.' Jane holds a bunch of papers up. 'Keep the details in your heads. It could be these two cases are linked.'

She gives the papers to a nearby constable. 'Hand these around would you, Rhys?' The young policeman hastily takes the posters and does as he is bid.

'There have been no other missing persons reported in the past three months so we will assume for now that our woman is not from these parts. Therefore, to start with we will look for missing occupants of hotels, B&Bs and rented places as well as women fitting the description who have recently checked out.'

A united breath is discharged by the gathered men and women.

The vast board is now covered in photographs of the cadaver, the cave and the clothing. Jane points to a photograph of the bruise on the back and then to another of the puffer jacket removed from the corpse. There is a close-up photo of a definite mark on the back of the khaki cloth where something sharp has prodded it hard.

'Forensics have explained that this bruise was caused by a pointed implement. On a hunch, they tested it against the end of a walking pole which fits exactly. That would be the end of a pole with a trekking tip for mountain use rather than a rubber ferrule. If we can trace the actual pole, it should bear some fibres of the victim's khaki puffer jacket. We just need to find it.'

The officers wriggle in their seats. She points to the photo of the remains of the face. 'I know it's a tall order but it is essential we find out who this is.'

She points to a picture of the necklace. 'This badly-corroded item is actually a silver chain necklace with a cross on it. So, at the moment, we are working on the person's identity and looking for the walking pole that we suspect was used as the murder weapon. I want a team up at the Cauldron searching the ground all the way round for anything they can find. Leave that to you to organise, Detective Warren. Okay?'

She delegates tasks to each officer and the station becomes a busier hive of activity than it has been for some time.

The staff and officers file out to get on with their work. She thinks they should move the vital members of the team up to Fishguard Police Station. They'll need to be nearer to the murder scene than they are now.

She tells Evans to call Fishguard to see what facilities they can offer.

Jane is back in her office but has left the door open around which Evans pops his head. 'Excuse me, ma'am, but Fishguard town hall has an unused room waiting for us to use. There's not enough space at the station. Hope that's okay?'

'Well done, Evans. Get the team together and we'll leave soon as.'

With a stab of panic, she remembers Meg. For as long as it took, Carys was going to have to step into Jane's shoes. In a case as important as this, the job simply has to come first.

Jane has planned an evening of carnal lust with Gareth but that will have to be put on the back-burner for now. A nice man with a good physique and a strong sexual drive, Gareth suits her just fine. He too is in the force, has been married and divorced and understands the demands of the job.

Wrongly perhaps, Jane realised a time ago that there is no way she will ever have a proper boyfriend again, let alone a live-in partner. For now, she wants nothing more than occasional sex with no involvement deeper than a physical relationship and Gareth is happy to go along with that. They're not even what is known as friends with benefits – they are simply casual sexual partners who enjoy one another's bodies. When together they make sure to avoid anything but small talk. So neither knows much about the other, although this does cause a hidden strain on both of them as it is an unnatural situation.

The temptation is in both of them to get to know one another better, but they struck an agreement the first time they slept together that they wouldn't. Instinctively, they are both attracted to one another. This is not just physical: they can feel the soul of the other shine through their sexual liaisons. They tell themselves that what they have is better than nothing, so they carry on as they are, looking forward to each time they meet.

It does not cross Jane's mind that she is a woman many men would treasure, and she cannot imagine that they would accept her lot as Meg's carer. She is convinced that no man could love her enough to accept that Meg's needs come first in her life. Since she parted company with her much-loved boyfriend after the accident, her thinking has been coloured. She hasn't allowed herself ever to imagine that things may change.

But Meg is now in her twenties, coming to terms with her disability well and already thinking about building a life for herself. Grateful though she is, her spirit still resists relying so much on others, in particular her sister. Just as she has had to work to recover from the accident, she has worked hard at and become highly accomplished at pushing away the demons that nag her to feel sorry for herself and to be angry at life for what it has done to her.

6

APRIL 2015. PEMBROKESHIRE, WALES

Mike had suggested they went abroad for Easter but after attempting to obfuscate the issue and giving various reasons why not, Bette had finally had to come clean that she had never had a passport. She said she had never tried to get one for fear her parents would have to be contacted or would find out in some way where she was. Mike had assured her he would help her with an application but she had become defensive and gone quiet and had said she had never wanted to go abroad anyway. Disappointed, as he had hoped to take her to meet his mother in Oz, he had let the subject go for now and decided to tackle it at some point in the future when she felt more secure as he was sure she would in time. Bette wanted to avoid the southern part of the county but was pining for some time in her old country so she had suggested an Easter walking holiday in north Pembrokeshire.

Pleased with the idea, Mike booked a hotel in the country-side between Fishguard and Newport.

On a sunny, challenging afternoon walk along the coastal path, they were entranced as they passed dramatic clifftops and zigzagged eastward, catching sight of occasional grey seals and a glimpse of a bottlenose dolphin. When they came to the rugged, convoluted rock strata around Ceibwr Bay, their path became trickier as it approached the remarkable place they had planned to visit. They stopped on the almost sheer sides of the Witches' Cauldron and gazed in wonder at such a natural curiosity.

Seeing a sign to somewhere called Moylegrove, their eyes followed the pointer and directly inland, perhaps 200 metres away, an old house stood alone on a level grass field. Drawn to take a look, they walked across the field, wary sheep stopping grazing to watch them. The big derelict house was built of solid stone. Ivy clambered over the crumbling roof. Battered and dirty, blown by the fierce sea-winds, an estate agent's 'For Sale' sign leant at such an angle that it was perilously close to toppling over. It had clearly been there a long time.

The size and state of the building would put many people off, but not Mike who knew what builders charge and how much a place can improve in worth once renovated. He was aware that a place like that with its astounding, remote, wild aloneness and amazing sea-views when well-renovated and nicely furnished would command premium holiday rental prices. But that aside, he was in love with the place and the idea of doing it up. He had the funds to buy the place four times over so there was nothing to stop him and it was a project he would enjoy getting his teeth into.

They tried the faded oak door but it was locked and they could see little through the dirty, cracked windows. The views were to die for and Bette knew then and there that they must have it. What she particularly liked was its isolation. There was not another building in sight.

They walked beyond it, following a lane a mile inland and came to a small unspoilt village where close-packed, colour-painted and stone cottages huddled along the sides of a hill. This was Moylegrove. It looked as though it had remained unchanged for many years and could not have had a population of more than a few hundred. They soon discovered that it was predominantly Welsh-speaking, which Bette was just about able to understand. They walked around and could find no pub and no shop. There was nothing to draw a tourist, apart, that is, from the coastal path and the Witches' Cauldron.

They approved of the place and set their hearts on their new venture. The ruin was such an enticing building that Bette and Mike took little time to persuade themselves into buying it. At that point, they realised the sun was sinking, painting the cliffs pink and yellow and they had to walk quickly westward to reach their hotel before darkness.

The following morning, after a hearty hotel breakfast, the two drove back to the ruin to meet a sleepy estate agent from Cardigan. With difficulty, the rusty old key sticking, he finally managed to open the creaky old oak door and showed them inside. The house was named Cliff Edge and they saw no reason to alter it.

The old flagstone floor thrilled them but the best thing of all was that the house had planning permission with stipulations attached. Mike knew his way around planners and that didn't worry him at all. They put in an offer that morning that was snapped up by lunchtime and returned to Cambridge the proud new owners of a house in Wales. Once back in Cambridge, Mike started on plans for the place that he knew would be acceptable.

Between April and September, the pair visited Cliff Edge almost every weekend. Bette, being her own boss, sometimes took days off from her interior design company to stay at the hotel they had stayed in when they had first found Cliff Edge and she'd be around during the week while a team of best Welsh builders cracked on.

By the end of September, the building work was completed. Mike had been careful to use local stone to fit with the planner's demands. At the end facing the sea he put in a floor-to-ceiling picture window to frame the spectacular view of grass fields dotted with cream sheep that stretched down to a ribbon of dark cliffs beyond which the vast blanket of sea took the eye to the horizon. He had added two more windows that were in keeping with the original ones and removed the old staircase and most of the ceiling. Now the open-plan kitchen incorporated the living room and an eating area and the old upstairs corridor became a wooden balcony with an attractive iron railing from which a winding iron staircase descended.

Above one end of the high space, he had designed a second floor with three double bedrooms. Downstairs, a wood-burning stove stood against one wall, its long, black flue pipe reaching for the heavens as it climbed up to the roof. It was much needed in the blistering winters.

For the summer there were the sliding doors on the end of the building, through which the patio was reached. This was where people would gather to eat food cooked on the brick barbecue and to take in the remarkable views across the sea and the Welsh countryside.

They kept the old, silvered-oak front door with its heavy iron handle, and the old porch became a place to hang coats. Although Bette had had a say in the design, Mike's attention to detail that could so irritate her at times was now put to the best use and she saw it as a big positive in this case. No wonder architecture had been his chosen profession. He excelled at it.

Bette decorated the place using soft colours and limed beams. She sought out solid, old, oak furniture, leather sofas, and old chapel pews became window seats with buff seat cushions. Two more pews were ranged either side of the old dining table. Everything had been carefully considered. She had learnt well from watching what others did and studying design and interiors magazines.

She painted the master bedroom in the shell pink she had longed to paint her childhood bedroom in. The second double room was pale blue and the third the palest yellow. They were simply furnished with old wardrobes and modern beds with soft-coloured covers and throws. Each bedroom had an en-suite bath, shower and toilet.

Both Bette and Mike enjoyed the work involved in getting the house renovated. They loved the area and relished the long walks along the coast.

Bette dealt with the bookings and a local woman, a Mrs Edwards, earned her share of the rent by changing sheets, cleaning, and making ready Cliff Edge for holiday lets when they weren't using it for breaks for themselves.

The first year they had rented it out, they put Mrs Edwards to the test by letting it to friends without telling her. The friends had reported the house as 'immaculate' when they'd arrived, with things exactly as they had asked. As instructed by Bette, Mrs Edwards always made sure to leave her contact details and offer any help she could give, including cleaning, cooking, ironing and babysitting. Bette had tried out some of the competition and made sure that new guests received a welcome basket on the kitchen table containing a small jar of coffee, some teabags, tiny pots of honey and marmalade, sachets of sugar, four small packets of breakfast cereal and some milk left in the fridge. People felt happy to be there.

According to the seasons, a local man took care of the grass around 'The Edge' as it was known and looked after the tall bank of evergreens which included a holly bush and various other large shrubs beside the patio, planted to lessen the impact of the wind that could blow hard off the Irish Sea.

For that time in Bette's life, she felt appreciated by someone for who she really was. Mike had many annoying habits, it was true. His fastidiousness extended to the way he was always smartly dressed: he was unable to flop in joggers. When wearing a jacket, he constantly buttoned and unbuttoned it. When he wore a tie, he frequently straightened it, and he was always touching his hair and checking his teeth. These were things that would normally have driven Bette mad and sent her running, but she ignored them in favour of his many merits.

Equally, Mike was as much in love as ever with this captivating woman. A keen shopper – not from eBay these days – she spent a lot of time in Cambridge's most expensive hairdresser, clothes-shopping in fashionable London boutiques and top department stores, taking taxis everywhere and spending far too much of his money, about which he always tried to be so careful. But he indulged her. She was young and at last had some security. She deserved his indulgence.

Yes, she could be a bit of a diva at times. Yes, she was unable to apologise and continually forgot what would wind him up (such as an unmade bed). Yes, she was tactless; she quite often put herself first and she was unpredictable and she refused to apply for a passport when they could have had so much fun abroad. But for him, these faults were completely outweighed by her beauty, charm, spontaneous laughter and by the way she made him feel he was the only person in her world.

Strangely, however outgoing and charismatic she was, Bette had few friends. In fact, when Mike thought about it, she had almost no female friends. But then, she hadn't been in Cambridge long and, after all, he had very few pals himself.

They were worlds apart and quite similar. Perhaps because they had moved in together so soon, the most basic thing their relationship lacked was trust. While neither gave the other any cause to think this, neither was certain the other was entirely trustworthy. They did both spend quite a lot of time working and both had jobs where they were liable to meet members of the opposite sex. They were both attractive people aware of their ability to attract others and this resulted in an underlying but well-hidden concern.

Tuesday 7th April 2015. Bette Davies' Five-Year Diary

Mike and I have found our Heaven. It is called Cliff Edge and we are over the moon about it. On the wonderful, wild, north Pembrokeshire coastline and we can see the sea from the windows. What could be better. We are as in love as ever and now I have somewhere to shout it from – the clifftops!

7

MAY 2016. KINGSWELL ROAD, CAMBRIDGE

One Saturday morning, Bette woke feeling nauseous and rushed to the bathroom to throw up. She went back to bed and lay there a little longer waiting for the feeling to pass. Mike had brought her a cup of tea and once her stomach had settled, she got up. Putting on her knickers before dressing, she had been surprised when the already-dressed Mike had shouted from the top of the stairs, 'Back in a brace!'

She heard him tearing down the stairs, almost tripping as he went, opening the front door and closing it with a bang. She went to the bedroom window where she watched him leg it up the street to Chesterton Road. Had he gone mad? Whatever was the man doing?

When he returned, Bette looked astounded. He was brandishing a pregnancy test kit.

'Don't worry, sweetheart. If it's negative, we'll be fine. Just one of those things. We've a long time to try again.'

'Why would you think I'm pregnant?' She was bemused.

'Because that may have been morning sickness you had earlier and that lovely little tummy of yours has grown as well as your breasts, which are definitely larger. I've noticed your appetite has increased, too.'

'Never!' was all she could say. 'That's just ridiculous.'

He gently handed her the kit. 'For me, my darling?'

She hesitated.

He dropped to his knees in front of her. 'Please? If you're not, it won't matter.'

She walked slowly to the bathroom, went in and closed the lock on the door. Privacy was vital at this moment. She sat on the lavatory seat for a time before she came out. Hovering by the door, Mike couldn't hide his impatience. When she finally emerged, she looked shocked.

'Well?' he said. He gently took the test from her trembling hand. He looked at the blue line. 'Oh my God! Oh God! My darling girl, this is fantastic!' He started dancing round the room. At that moment Bette felt as though Mike now had what he wanted and that she was simply a vessel to carry his baby. She sat down quietly on the bed watching him while she tried to get her head round what was happening.

'My mother will be over the moon.'

How could he bring his mother into this while she had no family to care? It wasn't as if the woman cared much about him since she had galloped back to Australia at the first chance she had had. Bette supposed his dependence on his mother might have had something to do with his eagerness to have children. Although he didn't behave in an especially jealous or possessive way, she sussed that having a child would make her that little bit less independent than she was now.

Could it be, she wondered, *that he doesn't like me doing so well in my business?* But then he had been starting to help her with it and recommended her to clients, so it couldn't be that.

She didn't think to remind herself that he was older than she and that perhaps his biological clock had started ticking before hers.

But Mike had seen this quite differently. Bette had made it plain that he had put his foot in it. In his high state of excitement he had forgotten her feelings. *Of course,* he said to himself, *she would be terrified of a test that might prove she wasn't pregnant.*

'I'm so sorry, Bette. I should have thought about how you might feel before I rushed off in such a hurry. It was silly of me and I apologise, my darling. Don't worry: if it's negative, it won't matter. We'll be fine. Just one of those things. We've a long time to try again.'

He had held her close. Without a word, she had showed him the test. He had smothered her face in kisses. 'My clever girl, my clever darling. Oh, I love you so much.'

He had been longing to put this into her mind but was scared she might not like the idea so soon and had given her a year's grace before doing so, adamant that a baby could only add to their pleasure.

In silence, she had crossed to the bed where she'd sat down slowly. For a moment he had wondered if she was upset. But he often forgot her down-to-earth Welsh roots, though they came to the fore in moments of stress. In the blunt and often funny way she had, she stared at the floor for a while before looking up at him and saying, 'Shook me rigid, that has.'

Mike insisted on accompanying Bette to all her maternity hospital appointments, including the breathing classes so he could better understand his role as a father on the day of the birth. At the first examination, the doctor said, 'I see you've already had a child, Bette, and this one will be much easier. Second ones always are.'

Bette went crimson and snapped at the doctor, 'I have never had a child before. Why would you would say such a thing?'

The doctor stepped backwards and stammered, 'I do apologise, Ms Davies, I fear I must be mistaken.'

The remark had obviously upset Bette. Mike supposed that anyone would be upset to have their history questioned. It did flit across his mind that she might have had a miscarriage when she was with her ex that was too emotional to mention. After all, she was not prone to discussing painful personal issues. He promised himself he would never mention the matter.

8

APRIL 2017. TRUMPINGTON, CAMBRIDGE

The exhausted, miserable, half-closed grey eyes of Sara de Vries roamed over the dirty dishes piled on the coffee table of the messy flat. From there, they shifted to the grubby, second-floor window through which they settled on the ugly incineration tower in the distance, rising among the vast complex of buildings of Addenbrooke's Hospital.

Just about everything had beaten her and it was his fault. Her angry brain ached for the loss of him, her dignity and for the job she had worked so hard for. She had been let go after a screaming meltdown when she had started to miscarry during a massage session.

It felt as though she had nothing left in the world. Negative thoughts overwhelmed her as she watched the tall, dirty brick monolith with the two huge chimneys, each topped with three outlets. She imagined herself a part of the smoke that drifted from the chimneys into a dull sky of welcome oblivion.

That is where I should be, she thought, *burnt to a smoky pulp along with afterbirths, aborted and miscarried foetuses, organs and body parts.*

But the part of her brain that was still in touch with reality knew she should be at a doctor's surgery asking for help. The time had come, she realised, to make the choice to live or die. And the part that was driven to stay alive was more than simply doing that. It knew she must carry on if only to get revenge by not allowing that man to be her downfall. The rage that churned under her depression stirred thoughts of actual retribution but she could not make the effort nor find the wherewithal to bring it about. Perhaps in time, she would. Where the next rental payment, due soon, was going to come from, she was uncertain. Since she'd stopped working, money was becoming a real problem.

An image of her mother came into her mind, eyeing her daughter and shaking her head in disgust. Sara shook her own head to clear the vision but the mother remained tutting and disapproving, hair scraped back, black dress rustling.

Dutch-born Sara had come from a small, isolated community of Calvinist people in a remote, traditional fishing town in the north of the Netherlands. Surrounded by sea on three sides, it was a poor place where the people had large families and the town was made up of only white Calvinists, no other races or creeds at all. Only an hour's drive north of Amsterdam where marijuana and prostitution were legal, it was a God-fearing town with more than nineteen churches. Some of the adults wore black, including her parents who dressed her and her twelve siblings in the same colour as well as covering the girls' small heads with white, lace-edged caps.

In that place there was little other for a man to work at but fishing or being a church minister. In Sara's case, her father was one of the few ministers which meant that the family attended church for three hours every Sunday, rejected television, radio, films, dancing and any displays of jollity. They were sober, reserved, conscientious, rule-driven and thrifty. This meant that they disapproved of just about everything to do with modern living and distanced themselves from it as far as possible. They even had a local dialect that was different from most Dutch. But with the high birth rate and a large youth population, the town had developed a problem among the young with alcohol and drugs.

Sara had been one of those who had discovered alcohol at the age of sixteen. A pretty, slim blonde, she had met a boy called Lucas with whom she had secretly drunk vodka and smoked marijuana, the thrill all the greater for its illicit nature.

Eventually, agreeing they had to get out of the place, they had quietly disappeared one evening and hitch-hiked to Amsterdam. Amazed by the place they had arrived at, they had been barely able to believe the city so full of life and lights, the canals, the red-light district and Dam Square with its colourful street entertainers and hawkers.

They found a rough place to sleep, sharing it with tramps and addicts. Before long, depression had begun to attach itself to Sara and she had started to feel full of remorse for leaving her family. She felt particularly bad about leaving the younger ones whom she had taken under her wing, protecting them from their mother's repressed rage.

Although fearful of the certain wrath of her parents and likely ostracism as community punishment, she had wanted to return. Lucas, on the other hand had desired no such thing. But then things had improved when they had found jobs, she as a waitress and he on a *kanaalboten*.

The first thing she did when she'd been paid was to go to a second-hand shop and buy some colourful clothes. The black dress she'd arrived in had been ceremoniously dumped in an open rubbish bin.

She began to adapt to her new life and, feeling renewed, had found a small, furnished studio apartment in a suburb for about 300 euros a month. This ate most of her income, but her newly won freedom felt so exceptional and the potential fun to be had so enticing that she had stayed. She and Lucas gradually drifted apart but she'd befriended a backpacking English student called Emily who was on a gap year and was staying for a few months.

After a time, Sara's deeply instilled guilt had decided she should give something back and since it couldn't be to her own, it would have to be to the greater community. Years of helping her younger siblings with learning had given her some pleasure in the role of helper, so she knew that helping others was what she wanted to do.

English language had not been encouraged in her Calvinist school so she decided to enrol on a course. She had bought a second-hand Dutch-English dictionary and found a cheap teach-yourself-English book and started to learn.

Because of the effort she made to speak English to Emily, they quickly became firm friends and started to spend every evening in one another's rooms. On one of these evenings, Sara asked her pal whether she liked her new dress, bought from a market stall that day.

'How can I tell if you don't try it on?' Emily had grinned.

'Okay then.' And Sara had turned her back on her friend while she'd slipped off her trousers and top. That was when she had felt Emily approach her from behind, put her arms round her and cup her breasts in both hands.

Transfixed by what was happening as Emily gently massaged her hardening nipples, Sara had felt a delicious, sweet feeling spread through her body. Emily had lowered her right hand to Sara's pubic area and slowly felt for her clitoris which was by now wet and slippery. She had eased her forward to the bed where she had brought Sara to the first climax of her life.

From then on, the pair had become inseparable. Then it had come to the time in September for Emily to go back to England to start at Cambridge University where she was to study music at Gonville and Caius.

Since Sara wanted to learn English, Emily had told her Cambridge was just the place as it had many language schools. She had first suggested then begged Sara to come with her. Coming from a well-off family, Emily had explained that she would have a good enough allowance to pay for Sara's lodgings until she found her feet in the town. She added, 'You'll be able to find a job to pay for your course.'

So they set off for Cambridge together and Sara was entranced by the old city. She now felt far enough away from her family – both culturally and emotionally – to really start life again. Amsterdam had been a learning curve of life without her family; Cambridge proved to be a place where she at last felt grounded.

The affair between the young women flourished for a few months but gradually waned as Emily began to find undergraduate friends and Sara did the same at her language school.

After a year of intense study, Sara, a diligent girl, working all the time to support herself, had become close to fluent in English. By this time, she had learned that she liked men as well as women. She had now moved in with a group of three other students. One girl had become a close friend with whom she had slept until the band of four had dispersed.

Sara became so devoted to the country she now lived in that in a sense, she became more British than the British. Her remorse at leaving her younger siblings made her determined to help treat and, if possible, heal others.

She worked hard waitressing and cleaning houses and flats to earn enough to pay for her courses. Gaining certificates in massage therapy and Indian head massage, she soon had a thriving little practice within a big sports centre in the heart of the city.

But today, so empty of energy that she couldn't have managed to massage a cushion, she realised she hadn't washed for ages and that she smelt bad. It took an intense effort to pick up her phone and select the contact number for her doctor. She was told, 'You need to call back tomorrow morning at 8am if you want an appointment.'

It took even more to wake up the following morning after the disturbed, unrestful night that had become her norm. The glimmer of hope that had prevented Sara from killing herself had provoked her to set the alarm on her phone to get up in time, and somehow she managed to be on the phone making her appointment at 8am.

Offered an appointment at 9.15am meant actually having to get washed and dressed. During the past few weeks she had had pizzas and food delivered to the flat and had never ventured outside what had become a cocoon of misery. She pulled on a long-sleeved, brown T-shirt, a shabby green cardigan, a pair of black trousers and some trainers that had seen better days. Her hair was greasy and unwashed but she struggled out of the flat, dragged herself to her elderly, small car and drove to her appointment.

The doctor diagnosed severe depression and gave her a prescription for anti-depressants and told her that in two or three weeks she would start to feel better. He also suggested counselling but the way Sara felt did not encourage her to speak to anyone about her feelings, least of all a stranger. She had kept those feelings under lock and key since early childhood and was not about to start revealing them now.

We sat together in the car. I was wide awake but the other person was so sleepy they could barely keep their eyes open. The car bumped

along down the potholed track to the cliff edge. Then they began to fall asleep and slumped forward onto the dashboard. I pulled on the hand-brake and the car jerked to a stop. Reaching into the glovebox for the torch, I got out of the car, walked round to the driver's side, opened the door, shook the driver half awake and helped them out of the car.

9

WINTER 2016–MAY 2017. KINGSWELL ROAD, CAMBRIDGE

To Bette's disappointment, Mike had barely touched her since he had learned of the pregnancy. She understood that he had longed for a child but why he had been quite so over-precious and wary of having sex with her she had yet to discover, believing his behaviour to be quite unnatural, especially for a man with a high sex drive. But he would not be drawn on the subject so she had little she could do but accept it as a fact.

Now she had only a month left before the due date, she and Mike spent their first Christmas at Cliff Edge before the baby was born. They invited an old university friend of Mike's to stay and although Bette was too far advanced in her pregnancy to go walking, the men explored the area on foot during the short hours of daylight. The rest of the time, when not cooking, the threesome played games of Scrabble, Monopoly and read books.

And a few weeks later, after an untroublesome pregnancy, the event of giving birth that on account of her impatience Bette had said she thought was never going to happen, did.

At the end of January, a baby girl was born. They named her Lucy and the small family lived in contented if exhausting Baby-land. Bette didn't fancy breastfeeding so Mike was able to share in feeding the child and became proficient at winding, nappy-changing and trying to rock her off to sleep, at which he frequently failed.

Excited, Mike contacted his mother to let her know she was a grandmother, he was hoping she'd say she'd be over as soon as she could, but she didn't. Asking her whether she could get over to see Lucy sometime in the next month, she said she was going on holiday to Hawaii and wasn't going to be able to visit for at least six months but asked him to be sure to send videos and photos.

The old resentment bubbled up in him. How dare she? How could she? He had never felt so angry with her in his life and shouted down the phone, 'Tell you what, mother, don't bother. Just don't bother. We don't want you anyway. Actually, since it's obvious you have no desire to see your only grandchild, I have no desire to see you – ever again, understand?' If he could have slammed down a receiver it would have been so much more satisfactory than pressing a button to cut her off but press a button he did with as much a flourish as he could manage. When she tried to call back a few times, he didn't respond. That was the last time he ever spoke to his mother.

By April, Bette was drained, as was Mike. With persistent determination the child cried day and night and whatever they tried failed to stop her screams. They dosed her for colic but it made no difference.

They rubbed Bonjela on her gums, but it didn't stop her yelling.

They took her for long walks pushing the pram on Midsummer Common, during which the little girl slept happily until the moment they turned the pram into the small hallway of the house and lifted her up, when she would start up yowling again.

In May, they took her to the doctor who could find nothing wrong. Becoming desperate, they longed for one uninterrupted night's sleep.

Then one night they had the best sex they'd had for a long time and both got a better stretch of sleep than usual, when Lucy slept through. At the baby's normal waking hour, 6.30am, Bette tiptoed to her room. Lucy was still asleep.

By 8am, there was still no sound and Bette asked Mike to check on her. But the baby was still asleep. Unusual though it was, he left her sleeping. She must suddenly have turned the corner into normalcy and he did not wish to question such a momentous thing.

But at 8.20am, before leaving for work, he went again into the child's bedroom and peered at her lying in her cot. He spoke her name, at first quietly then louder. She didn't stir. He crept to the side of the cot. He gazed at his daughter, soundlessly sleeping. He touched her cheek. Surely that would wake her.

But the cheek felt wrong.

He touched it again and it was cold. *How could it be cold?* Struggling to process this unnatural sensory information, he hesitated before dialling 999. When put through to the operator, he said quietly into his phone, 'Ambulance, please.'

While he waited, he couldn't look at Lucy. He shouted for Bette to come.

When the ambulance service answered, he again spoke quietly, 'Oh hello. Erm, excuse me, I'm not sure... I have a feeling... not sure my daughter is...'

The operator said, 'This is the emergency service. What is your emergency, please?'

And that was when he heard himself shouting, 'Help me! Help me! I don't think she's breathing. My daughter. She was sleeping. Help me, please! I don't know what to do.'

He was now screaming, 'My baby's not breathing!'

Soundless, Bette had picked Lucy up and was holding her close.

A calm operator asked Mike a series of questions. His mobile phone clenched between his face and shoulder, he followed her instructions, took Lucy from Bette and placed her on the floor. He told Bette to go downstairs and open the front door, ready for the ambulance.

Once he had established Lucy was not breathing, the operator talked Mike through how to administer CPR. He tipped her little head back, put his mouth over her nose and open mouth and breathed twice into his own flesh and blood. He depressed her soft little chest with two fingers, thirty times between breaths. He carried on with that routine until finally Bette brought the paramedics, a man and a woman, into the room. The man knelt on the floor and felt for a pulse. Then he set up a defibrillator with little pads he attached to either side of Lucy's chest. He delivered electric shocks to the teeny heart, checking in between to see if she was breathing. They tried a few more times then picked up their gear and took Lucy to the ambulance where the woman drove while the man carried on trying with the defibrillator. Bette went with them in the ambulance while Mike followed them in the car. He jumped into the BMW and stayed close behind as they put on the light and siren and raced across the city to Addenbrooke's hospital.

He followed the ambulance and when it drove up to the accident and emergency department, he saw the female driver jump out, run around the back of the ambulance, pull the doors open and help the man out holding his baby. They ran into the building with her and Bette on their heels.

Parking the car in a place reserved for hospital staff, Mike ran to the A&E. There were rows of cubicles, some that had drawn curtains, others that didn't. They were all occupied. His eyes wild, his hair dishevelled, he scanned the room but there was no sign of the ambulance crew or Bette and Lucy.

He ran to the nurses' desk and apologising to others queueing, barged in front, whispering, 'Where have they taken my baby? Tell me, tell me please.' When the nurse asked him to wait a moment, he lost all sense of decent behaviour and screamed at her, 'Tell me now, you fucking bitch. My baby was brought in here a few minutes ago. She was not breathing. I need to be with her, NOW!'

Realising she was about to be attacked, the shocked woman pointed to a cubicle. Mike followed the direction her finger pointed and tore across the room to pull back the pale-green curtains where the ambulance crew were waiting outside.

Lucy was immobile on the narrow bed. The silence was deafening. A nurse stood mutely beside the bed, small defibrillators in her hands while a doctor listened for a heartbeat through a stethoscope.

Bette, her hands holding her head as though it might fall off, stood at the end of the bed. She had no words and there was no expression on her face. She was clearly in deep shock.

The doctor knew he was only going through the motions. It was clear to him that the baby had been dead for some time. When he saw Mike, he asked if he was the father. On his confirmation, he was asked his name. He then attempted to lead Mike out of the cubicle to a private room where he could break the news, but Mike insisted on picking up the still little body off the bed. Her head, that he and Bette had recently been so thrilled she had learnt to hold up, lolled forward. He held Lucy close to him but there was no warmth, no sound, no movement. She was limp. She was dead. The light of his life was gone.

He said things to her, he whispered things to her, he sung things to her, but his words and songs went unheard.

The doctor pulled up the chair beside the bed and gestured

for both of them to sit down. The nurse gently took Lucy from his numb arms while the doctor spoke. 'Ms Davies, Mr Hanson, I am terribly sorry to inform you that at 9.43am today, your daughter was pronounced dead. We tried everything in our power to help her back to life. I'm so very sorry.'

Bette spoke. 'She's seventeen weeks old tomorrow.'

By this time, the hospital was following the rapid response protocol to a case of sudden infant death syndrome. The coroner and the pathologist must be informed as well as the police. The consultant paediatrician was at this moment examining the tiny body in minute detail for signs of injury or interference. Watching this stranger handle his darling made Mike intensely angry. It also made him feel as though he had done something wrong... that he had hurt Lucy or neglected her.

He thought back to last night. He suffered a spasm of guilt that he and Bette had had sex. It just seemed so wrong.

Lucy had seemed fine earlier and they had heard nothing through the baby alarm.

He pushed the invidious thought away.

Bette kept repeating over and over again, 'She was sleeping...' Tears rolled down her cheeks and when her puzzled eyes focused on Mike, she saw reddened, crazed ones staring back at her from a distraught face.

'She died, Bette. Lucy died.' He turned his face away, bent forward and bawled into his cupped hands.

Bette stood up. She lashed out at him and hit him across the head. When he stood up, she slapped him across the face and yelled, 'What have you done to her, you bastard?'

The doctor and a policeman glanced at one another. Mike put one arm tightly around Bette's waist and held her still. 'I have done nothing, Bette. Nothing that you didn't do. This is something that sometimes happens with no explanation.' He held her until she calmed down.

But Bette could only see Lucy's blue-tinged face and naked body with red patches either side of her little chest. This was the child she hadn't wanted.

She stood rock still, staring at her baby. Then, slowly, she crossed to the bed where she lifted and held the little corpse. She stood for a while in the same place, unmoving.

When this showed no sign of changing, the doctor put his hand on her arm and said quietly, 'Better put her down now, Ms Davies.' His soothing voice seemed to work and Bette carefully lowered Lucy back onto the bed. That was when the mother of the child fell to the floor, rolled into a ball and wailed.

After another twenty minutes passed where the parents sat beside their baby, each holding a tiny hand with their tightly-curled, shrimp-like fingers until the support nurse who had been with them from the start, put her arm round Bette and said, 'I'm so sorry but it's time to take Lucy away. You may both visit her again but it will be in a different place. We have to take her to the morgue now. I'm afraid there will need to be an inquest.' She addressed this to Mike who appeared to be more aware than his partner. 'It is likely this will prove to be a case of sudden infant death syndrome, the cause of which will probably be decided as "unknown". But in these cases, we have to be thoroughly careful that the facts are established. The police will want to examine your home as soon as possible. In fact, they would like to do so today, so would you please accompany Police Constable Morgan Tree who will drive you back to your house?' She looked embarrassed to have to say this. 'It's just protocol, I'm so sorry.' Then, she handed a leaflet to Bette who pushed it away. 'I think this might be helpful, Ms Davies. Perhaps you might look at it another time?'

The young police constable escorted Bette slowly to his car. He was red-faced from the horror of his first involvement with a cot death, and hardly knew what to say to the poor woman.

Fortunately for him, Bette had clammed up again. They got into his car and Bette rode in the back, stony-faced while Mike followed in his car which, miraculously, had not been towed away.

When they arrived back in their street, Bette guided the policeman to the house. Mike parked nearby and they all went inside. Their stomachs churned with the pain of the situation. They could not look at one another, nor at anything inside since the whole place now reminded them of what was lost. The young copper apologised profusely and stumbled over his words when he said, 'I'm really sorry but I am obliged to call crime scene – it's just procedure you understand – but they will need to examine the baby's room, cot, et cetera.'

'But we've done nothing wrong!' Mike was now enraged and squared up to the constable. Having to deal with traumatised people was bad enough and the young man himself was not unaffected by what he had seen in the hospital.

'Of course you haven't, sir, it's purely procedural. I wish it wasn't and I hate having to tell you this.'

Eventually, Bette pulled Mike back. 'He's only doing his job.' She was icy-calm again.

The crime-scene team soon arrived. Their work was meticulous. Everything was measured and photographed. The room temperature was taken, windows examined, furniture dusted, bottles, blankets, bedding, clothes – all bagged as exhibits. This took about three hours.

The distressed, grieving and exhausted parents now had to go to the police station where they were interviewed and had to make separate statements. The police also knocked on nearby doors to see if anyone had heard anything unusual the night before.

Once the twenty-four-year-old PC was able to finish that shift, he sat in his car, emotional and tearful. He knew the force deliberately sent childless officers to deal with cot death cases and he had no children himself. But he hadn't expected to be so affected and couldn't get the image out of his mind of the father with his arms outstretched, asking 'why' while the mother wailed, her head hidden within her hunched body on the cubicle floor.

∿

The masterpiece that had been the happiness of Michael Hanson and Bette Davies had disappeared and as a pair they now only worked on a superficial level. The initial agony of the police visiting their house, taking statements and photos of Lucy's cot was over. So was the horrible delay for the post-mortem result, during which their stomachs had heaved with the thought of what the pathologist had done to their beautiful little girl. The result was that nothing untoward was found.

In a sense, that made things worse for Mike and Bette.

He had never thought he would be squeamish about using the words 'death' or 'dead' but when it came to Lucy, Mike avoided them at all costs. For her it was 'gone' or 'her loss' or any of the terms people use to dodge the fact of fatality.

To have had a cause on which to hang the sudden death could have made the thing easier to come to terms with, but instead they were left with nothing to blame. Because of this they blamed both themselves and one another.

Mike had seen Lucy in the morning and hadn't realised there was a problem, but then Bette had checked on her in the late evening and in the early morning and had seen nothing to alert her either.

For the first three months, Mike was almost numb with grief. Not helped by time which crept pointlessly forward; everything became irrelevant to him, his own survival incidental.

Bette appeared to have taken it differently. She simply clammed up. At times, she almost seemed oblivious to what had happened but Mike knew she had donned the hard shell she had cultivated for so long to protect herself, against others and her own feelings.

Somehow, over the months they returned to some kind of forced normality. But they were going through the actions, they were making the gestures, they said and did the right things. But their mutual love had become a hollow memory, physically celebrating it a distant recollection and they now avoided touching one another as much as they could. At first, the distance between them made them even more miserable but they grew used to it and became happier with their own company.

Bette withdrew into herself but found it hard to sleep as her brain would not rest. She asked the doctor for and was given some strong sleeping pills.

Mike was depressed and this demonstrated itself in bitter antagonism. The more he thought about it, the more he started to wonder whether his partner had not been careful enough when checking the baby that morning. His mind churned with misery and that was how he was beginning to think of her, not by her name but by that distant, formal word.

His distorted mind looked back to why he had so loved her once and decided she had somehow tricked him into falling for her. He began to regret that he had been so eager to get her pregnant and more so that deep down his reasons for doing so had been based on jealousy. Perhaps his own guilt for enjoying the company of other women and flirting with them had exacerbated his own well-hidden mistrustfulness. *If I was Bette,* he thought, *I would have been suspicious of me, and the time I spent in the office with various females.* This had triggered his idea that if Bette's time was taken up with a baby, it would keep her away from contact with other men and work. Mike had seen the way they looked at his beautiful woman and lived in perpetual anxiety that someone would try to steal her away from him. He had never been happy with her working, especially in her job that involved meeting new people all the time. It had threatened his happiness.

He would always have preferred to have Bette waiting for him at home just as his mother had waited for his father. She had been so patient with the man who had always seemed to be either away or late home from his job. When finally he had run away with a younger woman, Mike's heartbroken mother had somehow found it within herself to forgive the man. This was the sort of woman Mike would like to have had.

But anyone with common sense could have told him that Bette was the last woman on earth who was ever going to follow that pattern.

If Mike could be called at all fortunate at this point in his life, providence did help him by landing his firm the major job of building a large, new, private school on the western outskirts of the city. This would put his company well and truly on the map and help make them very rich in the process.

In spite of his personal wealth, or indeed perhaps because of it, Mike wanted to prove he was as good as his dead father at making money and he now buried himself in the work.

Meanwhile, Bette didn't feel enough emotion to really care whether he was there or not. She resented that he had taken to coming home later and later. She didn't even bother to ask, but it did irritate her and she felt the loss of the devoted love he had had for her.

Her ego was badly damaged and she ruminated about what to do. Since she had lost the desire to work, she had taken to living off Mike's money and the prospect of being without that was not what she had in mind for the moment.

Mike's heart felt constant pain and the loss stirred his mind to believe the worst. At weekends he had taken to walking long distances alone, without ever inviting Bette to go too.

Staying indoors, Bette buried her head in books, reading more and more crime stories. They were all that interested her these days. Her interest in interior design had gone. Her website had become badly out of date. She had turned down work and lately it had dried up altogether. They didn't need the money so that was not a problem. The problem was how to find something to make life fun again.

They had never married but what happened to them had definitely put them asunder. They separately wondered would they ever get back that old feeling? Neither knew what to do about it.

25 July 2017. Bette Davies' Five-Year Diary

I am so sick of this ache. It's with me all the time. The missing Lucy ache I cannot get rid of. Some days it hurts a little less, so perhaps this means that in time it will fade but for now it drags me down. My heart hurts but I can't cry any more. I just wish I could. I feel it would help. But I can't. I'm too sad for tears.

Bette didn't want to continue being where she was or with the way things were, but she was stuck. She couldn't just run away. She had given up her rented flat and had no one to turn to.

That was when she had an idea. She was lacking companionship and missed being loved. When she recalled her childhood, the best companion she ever had had been the collie. That was when she decided to get another. That's what she needed. A collie in her life. She immediately felt alive again.

She surfed her computer for local breeders but then thought, *Why not get one in Wales?* That was where the best dogs came from. She made a call and a breeder she had heard of who produced good dogs happened to have a litter more than ready to go to new homes.

She also decided that if she was going to have a dog, because Mike was so fussy about keeping his car clean, she would need to have her own car for herself and the dog. Besides, it was time she had more independence from the man. So, she bought herself an estate car and drove it down to stay in a Swansea hotel overnight. That next day she drove to the breeder's place not far from Swansea. The pups were well overdue to leave their mother and were already house-trained. This was important as Bette knew the one thing that would aggravate Mike most would be a pup peeing on his immaculate wooden floors and white carpets. Even though he had long ago employed a cleaner since Bette had not proved good enough to keep his house to the standard he liked, a peeing pup would not go down well.

Having chosen the pup that looked most like her first dog, Bette brought him home with her that day. She naturally named him Brynn. The little dog immediately gave her the unconditional love she so missed and craved.

10

7 JANUARY 2018, 7.30AM. LLANGUNNOR TO FISHGUARD

Driving from her home to Fishguard that morning, Jane passes the Dyfed-Powys Police HQ building, that always surprises with its size. The enormous, red-brick, two-storey building looks incongruous sitting in what are usually green fields on the edge of Llangunnor. Today, although some snow has melted in the valley, pockets of slush remain and the landscape looks grey and dirty-white and messy. As she drives through the Welsh countryside, through villages and small towns towards Haverfordwest, Jane allows her thoughts to wander.

She goes around the details of the case so far. But she has learnt you can overthink a case and confuse yourself if you're not careful. So she forces her mind away from it and for some reason, probably sexual since she hasn't seen Gareth for a while, it takes her back to Swansea University where she studied criminology and criminal justice.

She sees herself in bed with the student she loved. That he loved her too was never in doubt. She remembers how her body tingled and responded to his touch and the swooning feeling she had experienced when their bodies had wrapped around each other and how they quivered together at the climax.

She wonders where that lover is now. Does he miss her? She certainly misses him. She wishes so much she could just talk to him, find out how he was. But when they had parted, they had agreed then to cut off completely as they knew they would never get over one another if they did not.

She sighs and decides to think of something other than herself. *What about Meg?* What love life lies ahead for her? She is so pretty and so much fun. There are boys out there who would love her but however could she get to meet them? Llangunnor did not have a lot to offer in that department.

There must be a way to help Meg be more independent. She has come to terms with her disability so well. Jane racks her brains and realises that although there are not many suitable men in Llangunnor village, there's a great big police station brimming with horny, young, single PCs.

She decides she will throw a party for her 23rd birthday in March. It will be at the station and she will invite the entire headquarters force. She began to cheer up after feeling rotten for thinking about her old lover. She would do her best to make 2018 the year in which Meg finds her metaphorical feet.

7 January 2018, 1.20pm. Pembrokeshire

As the team begin their search round the perimeter of the Cauldron, the wind has dropped which is a relief for all concerned, especially the police constables and sergeants who gingerly move on their hands and knees like four-legged animals stalking prey. They are studying every inch of ground as they go.

It is a wide net and constables have been sent to check on rental properties from Nevern to Glanrhyd and Moylegrove.

PC Rhys Roberts arrives back at the station. He was up early and has rung so many doorbells and knocked on so many cottage, farm and house doors that his knuckles hurt. But he has had what he feels was a successful morning. With only three more properties to visit before he had expected to return to Fishguard Town Hall with no information, he had struck lucky. Jane's office door will be the last he will knock on today.

'Come in,' she says.

He enters and shuffles on his feet while he waits for her to finish the form she is filling in. She puts down her pen and looks to him. 'Any news, Rhys?'

'Yes, ma'am.'

She raises her eyebrows and gestures for him to sit down. Jane listens carefully as the constable tells her how at a property near Moylegrove, a woman had opened the door with two dogs pushing at her legs. When he had put the question to her that he'd been asking all morning, she had seemed a bit uncomfortable. Roberts said he had seen a row of hooks in the porch on which hung outdoor coats and walking poles. He'd asked the standard questions, taken the woman's usual address in Cambridge and advised her to remain at the house the rest of the day as his superiors would want to ask her some more questions. Roberts had some nous and Jane made a mental note to bear it in mind.

'I smell a rat there, ma'am. The woman appears to be there alone which is strange. When I asked if the place belonged to her, she said she had been a guest of the owners over Christmas, and they had both gone missing. She had tried to contact them with no luck and hadn't known what to do since one of the dogs was theirs, so she had stayed in the hope they would return. Sounded very fishy, I thought. I think we should take a look. Oh, and by the by, I snapped a photo of her in case she tried to make a getaway. I also noted the number plate of her car.'

'Excellent work, constable.' Jane looks at the picture. She recognises her. She interviewed her three days ago about the missing woman who cleaned the house occasionally. *She said she was a guest of the owners. They were out that day. How come she's still there alone?* Now she or they may be associated with a death by drowning. Jane's antennae quiver with interest. 'Met this one before. By the way, I'd like you to come with us later, Roberts. Okay?'

Roberts grins broadly, unable to extract the excitement from his reply. 'Oh, yes... I mean, yes of course, ma'am. Certainly, ma'am.' So much more interesting than the usual drudge of paperwork, clearing road accidents and so on.

Jane buzzes through to Evans and asks him to find out fast as he can what rental agency deals with the letting and when he's found it to ask them whether the place is currently let or not, who owns it and so on. She suggests he tries the local ones first. 'So, crack on with that then and soon as we know, we'll get over there.'

Evans likes investigative work. It's his forte. He summons a few members of the force to help track down which agency lets the property and gives a local list to himself.

While Jane has a moment, she calls Meg. 'Hey. How's it going?'

'Not good, I'm afraid.'

'Why, what's up?'

'Now don't go being upset, Janey, but I fell out of the chair, see?'

'You *fell*? Meg? Oh God, are you *okay*? Did you *hurt* yourself? How in God's name? Was Carys with you? Why didn't you or she call me? Are you back in the chair safe and sound?' Jane's head spins. She feels entirely responsible for her sister and worries constantly about her welfare. It wasn't always easy juggling her job and caring for Meg but mostly it goes okay. It is only when things don't go smoothly that she finds it hard. 'Oh, I'm so sorry, darling, I'm bombarding you. Just tell me, lovely, are you *all right*?'

'Firstly, I'm all right so don't worry now but I've done something to my left wrist. It's very painful. Carys just popped out but she'll be back in a while and the doc's on the way now. I didn't call as I know how busy you are at the moment.'

'Was Carys there when it happened?'

'She'd just popped across to do something for her husband.'

Jane's voice was sharp. 'What time was that, then?'

'Oh, around two o'clock, I think it was. But don't worry, I'm just a bit bruised and the wrist's unhappy but I'll live.'

The sisters shared a fighting spirit.

'You in much pain, lovely? How in hell did it happen?'

It was explained that the doorbell had gone and Meg had manoeuvred her chair to the front door. When she had tried to reach the lock to turn the catch, the front wheels of the chair had caught up with the doormat and as she had tipped her body forward, she'd leant too far and fallen. She'd tried to stop herself from falling out but one of her legs had become trapped behind the footrest bar and over she'd gone, her wrist taking the brunt of the fall.

Meg laughed but Jane could tell she was trying hard to sound more nonchalant about the incident than she probably was. It must be frightening to be cast on the floor, in great pain and alone. Although she knew it was unreasonable, Jane felt annoyed with Carys for leaving her sister. And why hadn't she taken Meg straight to the doctor? She should have loaded the chair into her estate car, the car that Jane had partially paid for so that the wheelchair could fit in the back.

'I never did get to answer the door. The bell rang once more then whoever it was went away. When Carys came back a few minutes later, she couldn't get in as I was wedged up against it. Lucky you'd given her a back door key, wasn't it? Anyway, she helped me back into the chair and called the doctor right away.'

'Couldn't you use your mobile?'

'That's the thing, see, I'd left it on the big table.'

'Oh Meg. Not wise, not wise at all. Remember what I've told you a thousand times about keeping it with you.'

'I know, I know. But I knew Carys would be back soon. The fucking pain wouldn't lessen whether I was in my chair or on the floor. I was okay waiting.'

Meg had always liked to have the last word and had never been lightly spoken.

Their father, an electrician, and mother, a dental assistant, Jane and Meg had grown up in Radyr, a suburb north of Cardiff with a brother, Griff, six years younger than Jane and four years older than Meg. The family had been a happy one. Her parents set the bar with their kindness to others, their hard work, their care and love of their children and each other. Like most families, this one had not been perfect. Dad had been capable of extreme grumpiness, and Mum had an overfondness for shopping and a lack of care with money that used to aggravate Dad a good deal. A typical boy, as a child Griff was naturally self-centred, Meg an attention-seeker and Jane herself had a surfeit of ambition as well as a strongly stubborn and determined streak. The latter was to come in very useful in the future that lay ahead of her.

On October 5th, 2013 at about 10.50, Mr and Mrs Owen and Meg, eighteen years old at the time, set off to visit Mrs Owen's elderly great-aunt in Cardiff for her ninety-fourth birthday. They boarded an eight-carriage diesel train on the City Line at Radyr that took a quarter of an hour to reach Cardiff and they travelled at the back of the front coach.

At 11.06, a Cardiff train departed for Swansea. About two miles to the west, the route crossed over the mainline between

London and South Wales. The diesel train on which they were travelling should have been held safely at a red signal until the points were set correctly and the way was clear. But it passed the red signal and ended up running the wrong way along the mainline. It collided nearly head-on at a combined speed of about 130 miles per hour with the train from London to South Wales carrying 421 passengers.

No warning, no screech of brakes: there was just a huge deafening bang, and they were thrown about, carriages lurching, rolling and crashing.

As well as hearing the impact, Meg, who had been sitting with her back to the direction of travel, had felt it through her seat. For a moment or two, it had seemed that they might be all right, since the train had continued on its way. But then it had derailed and the wheels had ploughed over the sleepers and through the ballast beside the tracks until it had done a half somersault before crashing onto its side.

The high-speed train was a much more substantial construction than the smaller train, the leading car of which was totally destroyed. The diesel fuel carried by the smaller train was dispersed by the collision and ignited in a giant fireball that caused a series of separate fires in the wreckage of the carriages.

The drivers of both trains died, as well as twenty-nine others: twenty-four on the diesel and six on the high-speed train.

Sometime around three o'clock in the afternoon, while on the beat in Swansea, young PC Jane Owen had received an urgent call. Almost unable to string her words together, the shocked young constable had managed to phone her boss and explain what she had been told. He had unhesitatingly sent a police car to pick her up and race her to the University of Wales Hospital in Cardiff.

In the crash, Mrs Owen had died first. She had been violently thrown across the train and hit her head hard against a

94

steel upright bar before falling to the floor with others on top of her. Mr Owen was jettisoned onto the floor where, as the carriage rolled, suitcases and bags from the racks above hurtled down onto him, followed by people. His neck had been broken but he was still breathing when the rescuers had cut through the wreckage and got to him.

The rescuers had got Mr Owen into one of the first ambulances to arrive but he had died on the way to hospital.

They had then found Meg, unconscious. Because of her serious injuries, medics decided to put her neck in a brace, strap her tightly to a stretcher and winch her up into an air ambulance helicopter that could get her to the hospital faster than any of the muddle of emergency vehicles that were now banked up on the roads near the scene.

It was just after they got her out that a fire had engulfed the carriage. The fire brigade had done their best but it was a powerful fireball and burnt hard before they could put it out. The most seriously injured and those in danger of dying were moved first so Meg was one of the earlier victims to arrive at the hospital.

About ten minutes after Meg was rescued from the train, she had briefly recovered consciousness and been able to tell a nurse her sister's name and that she was in the Swansea police.

Their brother Griff was studying to be an engineer at a college in Swansea. Jane called and he came as fast as he could.

When Jane had arrived at the hospital, Meg had already sunk back into unconsciousness. Desperate, Jane asked whether her mother or father were in the hospital but in the chaos that followed the tragedy, no one seemed to know. That they were missing had soon become certain.

Somehow, the way people do get through terrible things, Jane and her brother had gone through the crisis and together the pair had howled with pain and grief. They had stayed at the hospital, hoping against hope that Meg would come around. When eventually she had done so, she had been in great pain and could not feel her legs. The doctors explained that she had sustained a severe injury to the lower spinal cord that had resulted in paraplegia. She would never walk again. Her right shoulder blade had fractured, the humerus dislocated and the surrounding tendons had been badly torn. She had broken her right wrist. She had lost a front tooth and bitten through her cheek but fortunately, apart from bruises and cuts, her head had escaped injury.

In the next couple of days, the blackened, dead bodies had been gradually brought into the nearest hospital morgue where relatives were invited to view them or if they were too badly burnt, to inspect the charred remains of watches, rings, wallets, handbags, jewellery or any other personal items that had survived the fire in their attempts to identify the victims. It had been a horrendous experience for the families who could smell the diesel and the smoke on the bodies and personal items. Jane had had to identify her missing mother by means of a charred bracelet and her engagement ring.

Jane and Griff had gone through the most horrible feelings they could imagine. Time had frozen, leaving them feeling like zombies who didn't know which way to turn.

Meg had had to become her siblings' main concern now. The grief they had felt for their parents had had to be contained when they were at her bedside. The doctors had agreed with Jane to delay telling Meg the full news about their parents. Since they didn't visit the hospital, obviously she realised something was up, but Jane had allowed her to think they were injured rather than dead.

There would never have been enough time for her to absorb the shock of what had happened to her, but inevitably the news had had to be broken sooner rather than later.

The poor young girl had subsequently sunk into a quagmire of despair. It had made dealing with her paraplegia doubly difficult. But in time and with the aid of tablets and counselling, Meg had sourced some fight in herself and once she had, a great deal of courage and endeavour had emerged.

Since the terrible accident that destroyed their lives, at the age of twenty-seven, Jane had to make a huge sacrifice to become Meg's father, mother, sister, carer and friend. Given a decent compassionate leave, she used the three months to get all the help the state could offer for Meg when she came out of hospital. She turned the dining room into a downstairs bedroom for her and the NHS had helped, adding a specially adapted shower to what was luckily a generous-sized downstairs toilet for the newly disabled girl.

Meg was in the hospital for six months where she had extensive physiological help as well as physiotherapy to teach her to do as much as she was able for herself, but that she was paralysed from the waist downward was undeniable. Her shoulder injury had affected a nerve that had made it difficult to use her right hand and meant she could not lift it higher than about twelve inches. In time, physio did help with that injury and very slowly she acquired more movement.

Unfortunately, Jane's boyfriend had fallen at the first hurdle and broken up with her. Deeply hurt though she had been, she had realised that such a man would never have been worth the having.

Griff did what he could but he was not yet working and Jane and he agreed he must somehow finish his course. Their mother's sister came twice a week to give Jane time off from this terrible burden and other members of the family stepped forward to do what they could. But after the initial horror of it all had eased, their help gradually waned. Jane didn't hold it against any of them as they had their own lives to lead. Social service's support was helpful but the truth was that it was still nothing near enough. Meg needed a great deal of care.

As the years have gone by, Jane has built a generally good system of care support that has meant she can continue to work. This is vital not only financially but for Jane's own sanity and well-being. She knows she would not have been able to bear caring for her sister for the rest of her life without something to escape to and she loves her work.

Her workmates have been extremely supportive of the enormous burden that has landed on her small shoulders. They are very fond of her and lost in admiration at how she has managed. On the occasions when Meg has had to see doctors or her specialist, they have stood in for Jane with no hesitation.

When Jane was offered a place at the Carmarthen headquarters as a junior detective, it had meant a rise in salary and an opportunity she had always wanted. She had sold the old Radyr house, given a portion to Griff and bought the bungalow in Llangunnor in which they now live.

Once Meg had come to terms with her fate, she turned out to be an excellent patient who seldom grumbled. She has adapted so well that she has managed to keep her strong sense of humour intact, and she shares the family trait of determination, inherited from their adored mother.

She remembers nothing about the crash. She doesn't recall being in pain, or afraid, or bloody and battered from the multiple cuts to her face and hands. But Jane remembers everything. Whenever anything happens to Meg it brings all the trauma back and she cannot help feeling anxious.

However light Meg makes of her fall out of the wheelchair, this phone call has reawakened all Jane's fears about her sense of responsibility for her sister.

11

SUMMER 2017. TRUMPINGTON

When, to her surprise, Sara looked back at the darkness that had encompassed her mind during her breakdown, she was not sure how she had got through those months of despair and the weeks of waiting for the pills to kick in. But the knowledge that they had helped her out of a morass of misery dared her now to believe that although she was not yet sure what, something good would come to her life soon.

Encouraged by her GP, she began to look for a new job with a clinic. There were no free positions going for a massage therapist and she didn't have the resources to rent a place she could work out of. But one clinic had suggested she should reapply after Christmas, since they knew someone was leaving in January. She was fairly certain she would be given the job and decided to go on Jobseeker's Allowance in the meantime.

The only thing that remained of her bitterness was the hatred she felt for the man who had dropped her. Most of the time now she watched television. One evening, a new advertisement appeared for a dog rescue place. This gave her an idea.

Now there she was, blonde head washed and shining, a lovely, long-limbed woman stepping out of an old grey car at

Wood Green near Huntingdon. Dressed in blue jeans and a pale-blue polo neck, that tall, slim woman walked into the main entrance to emerge about fifty minutes later with a pretty but nervous collie-cross on a lead.

A worker from the rescue centre walked with her as they gently led the scared animal round the grounds, giving occasional titbits and talking quietly to it in calming, soft voices. By the time Sara got the dog into the back of her car, it was starting to consider trusting its rescuer. They drove home and she felt happy for the first time for ages. 'Because you are female with an attractive long face and nose and you're both clever and brave in spite of your nervous disposition, I shall call you Virginia Woof.' There was a delay while she thought then added, 'But you'll be Gin for short. And I tell you this, Gin, life anew begins for both of us today. And if I have anything to do with it, it will be a good one.'

For a moment, she recalled the smell that filled her nostrils as she had attempted to wipe away the blood and amniotic fluid flowing down her legs. But the memory passed more quickly than usual.

'Lovely girl,' she murmured. The dog leant over the back of her seat and licked her ear. She had known the moment they met she was going to love this dog. What was more, she had known she would receive it back in spades for the rest of the dog's life. More than she could say for any man. All the ones she had ever met had turned out unreliable. She was sick of them. She thought back to her earlier lesbian experience and wondered whether that might be the way forward. At least women could talk. Unlike that last man who had finished with her. So repressed. He would never talk about his life, no matter how hard she had tried to get him to open up.

He had said he was a long-haul pilot who flew to America, Jamaica and Dubai from Stansted Airport. She had completely believed it at the time, but she now told herself she'd never believed it for a moment. He was just not like she imagined a pilot to be. She was now sure he had been lying to her all along. She caught herself raging again and then stopped herself. She must concentrate on her new charge.

It would take some work to get Gin used to normal life. This was good. It would give Sara something other than herself to think about. And in time the dog would relax and start to enjoy life again. Sara congratulated herself on the idea. For now she would concentrate on the dog.

Score settling could come later.

12

6 OCTOBER 2017. MAGOG DOWN, CAMBRIDGE

Named after the cannibal giant, Gogmagog, twin hills called Gog and Magog, are divided by a busy A road that leads from the south to the city of Cambridge. These gentle slopes are supposedly the highest hills in Cambridgeshire above a city on a plane that merges north into the dead, flat country that is the Fens. Magog Down is where dogs can run free and get a decent walk.

One surprisingly warm, early October day, the temperature around eighteen degrees, a pretty, blonde young woman drove about six miles out of Cambridge until she reached Magog Down where she turned into the car park. She got out of the car, walked round to the boot which she opened and grabbed a collie attached to a lead. The excited dog jumped out and the pair crossed the road. They walked to the first paddock where she let the dog loose. It immediately ran up to another smaller dog that was sniffing about in the field.

The two owners, both blonde women, watched the pair of dogs chase one another in circles. One turned to the other. 'What a beautiful dog you have there.'

'Yes, indeed he's gorgeous,' said the younger woman. 'So is yours. Will she mind me saying hello?'

'Well...' The other owner faltered and seemed taken aback as though that sort of thing didn't happen to her. 'But she's a timid one. Rescue dog. She's gradually learning to relax more. I don't know what happened to her. You'll need to go gently.'

The younger woman decided the dog's owner was older than she, probably by ten or eleven years. She squatted down on her haunches to the smaller dog's level, bowed her head and avoided looking in her brown, untrusting eyes. Murmuring sweet nothings, she put out her hand and let the nervous animal sniff her. In no time, she was stroking the dog's head and tickling its chest. They had made friends.

'Most people don't even ask,' said the older woman. 'They intimidate her by going straight to pat her and she'll either shy away or nip in fear. What a natural you are. Where did you learn such a knack?'

The younger blonde rose from her crouch to see wide-apart, grey lozenge eyes in a broad face with striking cheekbones. She supposed this woman might be called beautiful. There was something Scandi about her looks and the slightest hint of an accent. Her hair was bunched at the nape of her neck and tucked under a floppy hat. Close up, she could see it was light blonde and guessed it was as long as her own. She beamed broadly at the woman. They walked together across the small grass paddock towards woodland.

'I grew up on a sheep farm with collies. I know how nervous they can be. You get that in the breed. Some are plain neurotic. I can see the collie in this one. A cross, I imagine. What do you call her?'

'Virginia Woof,' said the woman, 'I couldn't resist the pun...'

Virginia. What kind of pretentious name was that? What's more, for a collie? Where she came from, they were called short, sharp names like Bel, Gyp, Rhys – words that can be easily heard across a windy field.

'...but she's known as Gin,' continued the woman.

Relief; that could be handled.

'And what a delightful boy,' continued the older woman. 'A sweet beauty he is. What do you call him?'

'Brynn,' she replied, bending down to stroke Gin again. The little crossbreed was also beautiful but had that highly-strung look about her that shepherds both distrust and avoid.

'Brynn and Gin. How funny.' The women walked together to the end of the meadow and turned left onto a path that led into a copse. 'So where was the sheep farm, if you don't mind me asking?'

'Pembrokeshire in Wales.'

'Oh how wonderful. You must miss it.'

'I do, but my partner and I bought a deserted old house on the north coast that we've made habitable. We try to visit as often as possible. We're keen walkers.'

'I envy you. I've never been but would love to go some day.'

'You should,' said the younger woman confidently. 'You won't regret it.'

'Does your family live up there?'

'My parents have both passed on and unfortunately I was an only child.'

'Oh, I am so sorry. How dreadful for you.'

'Shit happens.' She offered her hand. 'I'm Bette. You are?' Bette had learned the blunter the better and never skirted around telling people her mother and father were dead. It back-footed them and generally ensured they dropped the subject. It was much easier than having to go into explanations. Fortunately, the woman let the subject go. Bette flashed her charismatic smile.

'Sara.' Taken aback by Bette's use of the word 'shit' when

they had barely met, the woman gently took Bette's proffered hand. 'Nice to meet you. I'm originally from Holland. I'm an only child too. My father departed a few years back and my poor mum suffers from Alzheimer's. She's in a home and doesn't even recognise me when I visit. Strange not having parents or siblings, isn't it? Reminds one of one's own mortality.'

Bette wondered whether departed meant left or died. Undeterred by tact, she asked.

Sara looked down as though in deference to his memory. 'Sadly, I meant he passed on.' From her demeanour and the way she looked at her hands, Bette decided that Sara was clearly a private person and that she should watch what she said.

'What do you for a living?' asked Bette.

'I'm a massage therapist and Reiki practitioner.'

'Day off?'

Sara smiled. 'Yes. I'm my own boss so can pick and choose when I work.'

'Me too.'

'And may I ask what you do?'

'I'm an interior designer. I'm not working quite as hard at the moment as usual. Can afford to be picky about which projects I take on. It's quite liberating.'

They discussed their lives as they strolled along together towards the top of the down, the dogs chasing each other round the woods. Sara asked Bette more about her holiday place in Wales and talked about her own beliefs in healthy living. While Bette appeared interested to hear how much store Sara put in not eating certain foodstuffs such as butter, carbs and red meat, it was feigned. Her Welsh upbringing had ingrained dairy produce and lamb as the norm and she held no interest in challenging that custom.

At the end of the walk, Bette suggested that since they had got on well and the dogs had worn one another out, they should meet again. There was something about Sara that smacked a little of desperation. She seemed eager to befriend Bette who had a sharp radar when it came to analysing others. She decided Sara was a people-pleaser, a non-confrontational woman with little inner strength or self-belief. In other words, that the woman was weak. Correct in her perception of the impression Sara gave, Bette was not aware of what lay behind that impression. She was, in fact, altogether wrong.

What started that day soon became a regular thing. The women often drove out to the down. Sara was, seemingly, free most days. Bette also was seldom busy since work had dried up that summer.

On a wet day in late October, walking on a country estate on the other side of the main road from Magog, they plodded together through dank, dripping woodland. Sara confided that earlier that year she had suddenly and inexplicably been ditched by someone she had loved deeply. She had then miscarried his baby.

The woman had had to stop and sit on a fallen tree trunk where she had explained how tragic the loss had been to her, made worse because she had decided to keep the child.

Shocked, Bette said nothing but sat down next to the weeping woman, linking her arm through hers and squeezing it tightly in a show of understanding and affection. Sara grabbed her nearest hand and pressed it back. Then she kissed Bette on the cheek and let her head drop onto her shoulders. For a moment Sara then lifted her head and tried to look Bette in the eye. Bette wondered whether the woman was a lesbian but dismissed it as she knew about her affair with the man and put this ultra-show of affection down to gratitude and loneliness.

These past events had apparently spiralled Sara into a depression from which she was still recovering, and thereafter she had found she had been unable to cope with such a physically and emotionally demanding, client-facing job. There was a bitter edge to her words. Her experience had gone deep. Something apparently stopped Sara from finding an easy way through life.

When Bette tried to get her to open up, she clammed up. Bette knew well how the inclination to repress things is easier than having to discuss them. But still, she pushed her new friend. Was it, in some way, her alter ego she was really getting at? She wondered what Sara now did with her life but there was something so guarded about the woman that even Bette felt she couldn't ask. The opposite to herself, Bette was thought of as outgoing although that was only in a certain sense, for she was more of an introvert than people believed. She had learned to mask it as she had realised when young that it wouldn't help her get along in life.

'How did you meet?'

'He came to my practice as a patient needing massage. His back was giving him problems. We kind of went on from there. Oh, I know it was thoroughly unprofessional but he used to book in as my last patient and we would make use of the massage bed. Later on, as it became a serious thing, he would come to my flat.'

When Bette enquired how long the relationship had lasted, Sara had said it had been for about ten months. Surprised she couldn't have by now picked herself up and carried on, Bette decided that this seemingly normal, people-pleasing woman was a lonely, nervous person. Apparently, this had been the first time Sara had ever fallen deeply in love.

'What was so special about him?' Bette asked.

'Oh, he was intelligent, interesting and loving. I can't say exactly... he was very good-looking...' She shook her head. 'It's hard to talk about. It still hurts too much.'

'And he knew you were pregnant?'

'No. I was planning to tell him when I was sure at twelve weeks. But he ditched me a month before. That was soon before I miscarried.' Her face pained by these intimate questions, Sara rubbed her temples intensely to try to rid herself of this horrible memory.

'He sounds like a bloody rat.'

'I suppose, after all, he must have been. He certainly didn't seem like one. I don't know whether he'd have done that if he'd known about the baby.'

'Rats never seem to be rats; they don't look like rats, they don't even smell like them until you really get to know them.' Bette watched the poor woman who, head down, was holding back tears.

'Perhaps he was married?'

'Oh no! Definitely not.'

'Did he ever invite you to his home?'

'Well, no, he didn't, but he was away a lot, you see.'

'In that case, he was using you. He was only after you for one thing.'

Sara burst into tears again and Bette realised she mustn't go too far, that she'd better leave the subject of the rat alone for now.

Bette had been surprised to discover that Sara had a sense of humour and was relieved when together they had hooted with laughter about how they had both changed their lives. Their shared experience and the coincidence of their lives did seem somewhat extraordinary.

But Bette saw that although Sara may have been all right on the surface again, she was still unable to come to terms with what had happened. She believed her boyfriend had left because she was not fun enough or attractive enough to keep him.

The women had become close but Sara didn't invite Bette to

where she lived, nor did she seem willing to even discuss where it was, beyond that it was in the south end of Cambridge. The non-existent invitation was happily reciprocated. Neither woman wanted anything to spoil their neutral friendship in which there were no comparisons made about where they lived, their levels of income or their lifestyles. They were happy to leave their friendship in its own bubble, unadulterated by the pressures of the material world.

In a sense, the friendship was similar to the relationship some women have with their long-term hairdresser. They acted both as one another's listeners and counsellors. Although Sara hadn't struck Bette as a person who would mind what people thought, she could only imagine the woman might be embarrassed by where she lived. Bette had once asked her whether she lived alone and Sara's answer had been snappy.

'I certainly do.'

Bette had crossed her line and Sara hadn't liked it. Bette imagined a chaotic, small suburban house or flat. *Perhaps,* she thought, *Sara couldn't bear to take people back to her home because she hates them to see what a real mess her actual life is. This way she can at least keep up some pretence.* Bette imagined that many therapists are probably not well-off and judging from the state of Sara's ancient car that she had bought second-hand seven years ago, she never had been.

So Bette made an early decision never to enquire about the whereabouts of Sara's home, and she never hinted that she would like to be invited there. She didn't want to lose this friendship. It had become vitally important to her.

When she guessed at the sort of place Bette might live, Sara was closer to reality. She thought her friend probably lived in a tasteful, expensive house with immaculate décor, interesting artefacts and pictures dotted about. She presumed the popular shades of expensive paint on the walls, though she failed to envisage the dark-blue shade that Mike had picked, but that was not Bette's choice and nor was much of the décor of the house.

Sara and Bette were both beautiful blonde women who loved dogs and walking. But the similarities stopped there.

Where Bette was loud and sometimes brash, Sara was quiet and self-effacing. Where Bette could be called pushy and determined, Sara came across as non-confrontational and a person who would do much to keep others happy.

Bette had quickly taken the lead as the one who called the shots. That being said, there was more to Sara than met the eye and under that soft exterior lay a hidden capability to be cunning as well as devious.

The next time they met was what Bette called a watercolour day. The leaves and berries in the woods on the down starred in magnificent colour below the palest of suns just visible behind bulging clouds that appeared glued into place on soft blue skies. Bette decided it was a suitable day to tell Sara about Lucy. She had never talked about it to anyone but she wanted Sara to know. She felt she needed to redress the balance by putting Sara in the true picture.

'I loved my job and then I fell pregnant,' said Bette. 'It was sooner than I had wanted to have children. But my partner wanted them as soon as possible and kept pressing me to stop taking the pill. Anyway, as soon as Lucy was born, I fell in love all over again. I had never felt like that before and couldn't believe how strong my love was for that little mite. It was all-consuming and I completely adored her. I suppose I shouldn't say it, but I was the most devoted mother, absolutely besotted with that little angel. Then, when she was just four months–' A break in her voice and she stopped. Her head drooped.

Sara had the sense to remain quiet.

Finally Bette shrugged. 'It was confirmed as sudden infant death syndrome. That's it. I can't talk about it now and never will. I just feel hollow. Simply hollow. Like the frame of a person with nothing inside. But that frame will never stop aching. Never. Life since that day has been the most desperate and frightening time. At times it has been unbearable. I couldn't believe that a healthy baby could just die. I was convinced I must be responsible in some way. I remember thinking, *It's my fault.*'

Bette's eyes welled and she looked away as tears cascaded down her cheeks. Sara held her while she wept on her shoulder.

6 October 2017. Bette Davies' Five-Year Diary

Met a lovely woman today called Sara on Magog who I hope may become a good friend. She too has a dog and we had a lovely walk together. The dogs got on extremely well and we have agreed to meet again soon. It would be great to have a female pal in Cambridge. I really am in need of someone as Mike is no longer my soulmate. I miss him so much but I have lost him along with L. He has turned against me. I know it is because, like me, he is so unhappy. He seems to hate me. Always so angry.
One day I wouldn't be surprised if he doesn't do away with—
No, I won't allow myself to think it, let alone write it down.

13

19 NOVEMBER 2017. TRUMPINGTON, CAMBRIDGE

S ara was feeling low again. She was just recovering from one of the migraines that had started when she'd left home. They knocked her for six for a couple of days and she generally had to take time off to sleep in a darkened room. They had become rare until he had broken off their affair. Since then they had started to come back more regularly.

When she got like this, she had a tendency to overthink, convolute everything and dwell on her unhappiness. She recalled her childhood town, never able to obliterate those memories.

One of the main memories was walking with her mother who was wearing a boxy white cap that covered her ears. She had a plaid shawl around her shoulders over a long black dress. Her father in a dark suit was beside them as the family hurried to church for one of the three Sunday services.

In the church, she felt her knees rub against the rough prayer cushions as they prayed together in their black clothes.

She sat again at the kitchen table with her family while Father read the Bible before and after every meal. The Bible, the only truth in their world. She knew her family were known as 'black-stockings' in reference to the clothes the women wore. They lived for God who only approved of Christian music, who disapproved of gays, drunkenness, immunisations and insurance... and, apparently, laughter and fun. These things, she was taught, were in opposition to the perfection of God who was the only one to know what was good for his children.

When a child herself, she had been taught to feel guilt for wanting to laugh, for wanting to run and play, for wanting to enjoy herself. No matter how good she had tried to be, she had felt constantly disapproved of, and self-reproach had been ingrained into her along with introspection.

Sara felt that old familiar ache of shame for deserting her sorrowful family. She remembered and grieved for all her siblings and for leaving them behind. She tried to think of her mother with that same sympathy for inflicting the loss of herself on her. But however bad she felt for what she had done, she could not feel sorry for her. This woman who, for the sake of conformity and pleasing her community and her husband, had put her children through a life of guilt-ridden unhappiness. As so many others in that town had done also.

Now, though, Sara had another reason to feel bad. No matter how hard she tried to imagine otherwise, she was jealous of Bette. Why, she asked, did she feel like that? *Because Bette has a man,* she answered herself.

The neurotic insecurity now enveloped her, making her feel even lousier. Poor Bette, she knew, was far worse off than she; not wealth-wise, that was certain, but the hurt her friend had experienced was definitely crueller than her own. She felt bad too because even though their new friendship had become a lifeline to her, she had in a sense profited from someone else's misery. The onus this put on her made her want to help Bette over the stile to the next stage in her recovery. She tried to think what might help.

Surely it would be an idea to sell the house the baby had lived in. It must hold some terribly sad memories of that loss. She made a note to suggest it. Also that perhaps it would be an idea for the couple to get away from Cambridge at Christmas. Perhaps they should go to that place of theirs in Wales. A change, the brilliant scenery and walks in the sea air with Brynn could only be good for Bette and her partner. It might even help her marriage which sounded as though it was unlikely to recover from the huge blow the couple had endured.

Sara wondered why Bette never spoke about her partner. She realised she didn't even know his name. Could this be because Bette herself didn't want to think about him? *But why?* She pondered this and wondered whether Bette might in some way blame him for the baby's death. She had never hinted at this, but then she had never told Sara anything much about her marriage. Even if she was married. Sara did find this rather strange.

Much as she liked the charming Bette, she was not exactly easy to get to know. But then, Sara remembered, neither was she. Perhaps that was why they got on so well. Peas in a pod, happy to share a pod but to remain firmly in their own skins and attached to their separate compartments.

As she forced herself to take Gin out for a short walk on the lead, all it would be that day, her spirits lifted a little and she resolved to speak to Bette about her ideas when they next met. That time came later that week.

As she and Bette strolled over the top of Magog hill, Sara tentatively asked, 'I wonder whether you have contemplated selling your house. Might it be an idea to start afresh somewhere else?'

For the first time since they had met, Bette was clearly annoyed, even angry. 'We're perfectly all right where we are, thank you.' She quickened her pace and stumped along ahead of Sara, her angry figure speaking volumes.

'I'm so sorry. I've clearly upset you, Bette. It was the last thing I intended.' Sara half jogged to catch up with and keep alongside her. 'Forgive me. It was none of my business.'

'No,' said Bette who seemed a little less cross now, 'it wasn't.' She sighed and shrugged her shoulders. 'But you were only trying to help, I know.'

They walked on in silence for a few minutes before Bette stopped Sara, turned to her and beamed her lovely smile. 'So sorry, Sara. Sore point. Hope you understand?'

'No, no, it's me who should be sorry. I shouldn't interfere, I had no right.'

Contrary to what she had imagined, the couple obviously felt tied to the place that had been the only home their child would ever know. She changed the subject. 'Any plans for Christmas? I was wondering whether you were going to Wales?'

'Always wondering, aren't you, Sara?' Bette replied, the brusque edge back in her tone.

Sara simpered. 'I thought it might be a nice getaway for you.'

They walked on a few more paces, Bette deep in thought when she said, 'Actually, that's not really a bad idea. In fact, I might just do that. I'll suggest it to my partner.'

Still the nameless partner, Sara noticed. She presumed Bette found it easier to distance herself from him by not referring to him by name. She stopped walking and waited for Bette, who was ahead of her, to turn.

When she did, Sara slowly approached her, her arms wide in readiness to hug her friend. Bette seemed happy for her to do this and in the warmth of their embrace, Sara brought her head close to Bette and kissed her friend's pretty mouth.

Bette quickly sprung back. 'Got me wrong on that one, Sara. I didn't have you down as a dyke. Thought you liked the boys.'

Red with embarrassment, Sara hated being called a dyke. She didn't care to consider herself as such. This was the first time since all those years ago in Holland that she had touched another woman. She couldn't forgive herself but nor could she forgive Bette for making her feel foolish. She went quiet and kept her distance from Bette as they walked back to the car park. When they parted, Bette smiled at her. 'Chin up! It won't affect our friendship, I can assure you, Sara. See you Monday?'

Later, when she got home, Sara congratulated herself on planting the seed in Bette's troubled mind. Now she just had to hope...

It was made of aluminium. A good implement to smash over a head.

'How fucking dare you lie to me? See what happens, you deceitful, fucking, lying degenerate, when you do? This is what happens,' the manic voice yelled as the blows came down. 'This!' Blood spurted from the side of the head. 'This!' Bone cracked on metal. 'And this!' The frontal lobes took the brunt.

The raging words fell on the auditory cortex that was the last of the brain to die.

14

15 DECEMBER 2017. CAMBRIDGE

Mike and Bette were sitting in their normal chairs, not talking as usual, when Bette suddenly said, 'How about spending Christmas and New Year at Cliff Edge? We haven't been up there for ages. There's no one renting it, I checked with the agents.'

He looked up from his book. 'Suppose we could.'

It would be the first time for quite a while that Mike could get away since he had started work on the biggest project of his life, the private school on the outskirts of Cambridge. If he had felt better about life, it would have been very exciting for him. It was sad that the breakthrough he'd been waiting for had come at such a bad time in his life.

He could now do with a holiday to unwind and recover from what was turning out to be a stressful and long job. The fact that it had taken up so much of his working time had helped him more than he knew to begin to face life without Lucy. The problem he had was that every time he looked at Bette, she reminded him of that night and the trauma and guilt rose within him almost to the point of nausea.

I'd have to spend all the time with her, he thought. *At least in*

Cambridge, I can get away. Then he remembered the walks. *Ah, the walks.* He could go off for hours alone and get away from her quite a bit. She did like walking, but not to the extent that he did: he was happy to do twelve- to fifteen-mile hikes on a daily basis. And since the change in their relationship, she had stopped wanting to walk with him anyway. *She can stay in the house with her books,* he thought, *and she can cook and draw...*

She broke that train of thought by adding, 'I wondered whether you'd mind my inviting Sara, the friend I've made walking Brynn? She also has a dog and is a bit sad as she lives alone, has no family here, hardly any friends and recently got dumped by her boyfriend. I just feel sorry for her being alone at Christmas.'

He sighed with relief. It was just the result he could have hoped for. It would keep Bette happy; and would be someone to break the miserable silences that had become the norm for them. Besides, it was time she made a friend. 'Why not? Be a kind thing to do and in the spirit of the season, et cetera. Good idea. Ask her.'

Phoning Sara that evening, Bette transferred her enthusiasm to her friend. 'It'll be such fun, darling. We can walk the dogs in total freedom. It's so beautiful and wild up there. I know you'll just love the place and it'll be so good for you. Dogs'll love it, too.'

'Bette, you know I can think of nothing better but I feel you and Mike should be together without anyone else.'

'Capswabble! Mike and I don't want to spend much time alone. You'll be doing us both a favour. Just say yes, silly, and let's hear no more about it.'

'Put it like that, how can I say no? Except what *did* you actually say?'

Bette giggled. 'When I talk about Pembrokeshire, I do that

sometimes. Go back to the old ways, you know. Capswabble... It means nonsense.'

They chattered happily on about arrival times, routes and what to bring. 'Your warmest gear,' said Bette, 'As it's always chilly and windy on the coastal path and apparently, we're in for a cold front over Christmas. So it's quite likely to snow and you may have to watch you don't get blown off the cliffs... But seriously, it'll be huge fun and I'll look after you. Don't you concern yourself with anything except making sure to get there. By the way, I've got loads of spare warm clothes there so don't worry too much about that: you can always borrow mine.'

Sara put her mobile back on the edge of the sofa where, as usual, she was sitting alone watching television. She stared at it for a while. How well she had done. She had made it sound as though Bette's idea had surprised her, when in fact, of course it was her own idea, perfectly planted in Bette's mind. Her plan to get invited to Wales had worked, too. Everything was going just as she had hoped it would. She could now really look forward to Christmas.

Mike and Bette were now both off the hook about spending the long holiday alone together and neither of them could have been more relieved. They had been quietly dreading the time off. In fact, now Mike thought about Wales, which they hadn't visited since last Christmas, he began to really look forward to seeing the place again. Perhaps, he even dared to hope, it might help repair their marriage to some degree.

Since Lucy's death, he had taken to spending as much time as possible away from home. Every time he walked through the front door and went into the living room, the trauma of her death flooded back to him.

The memory of breathing into the tiny cold mouth, the difficulty of not putting weight on her in case it hurt her and of the horrible silence in the room when all he wanted to hear was her cry, haunted him.

He experienced regular nightmares of Lucy crying and in most of the dreams, he could not reach her or if he could, was unable to help her. He would wake sweating in the middle of the night to realise that she was not alive to cry. What he would have given to hear that sound again could not be underestimated.

His misery followed him wherever he went. He had secretly visited the doctor in despair as he had experienced the hopelessness the parents of deceased children feel. The doctor had recommended grief counselling but that was not a thing Mike would go for. He felt it was an intensely private matter and could not see how talking about such a miserable event and dragging up the blame and horror of it all would make him feel anything but worse. After a few weeks he had begun to feel more able to cope with life than before. But it remained empty and he ached and ached for the child he had so longed for and lost so fast.

The few friends they had had disappeared from their lives. They had no desire to see or speak to any of them and their lives became hollow memories of the real thing.

For some reason Mike had not been able to explain to himself, he had taken to using prostitutes. All the desire he and Bette had shared in the bedroom had disappeared in a second after Lucy died. Neither had any wish to touch the other. The prostitutes finally allowed his masochistic side to surface but they were not so much there to assuage his sexual needs as these had more or less evaporated, but more to remind him that he was still able to operate as a man even though sometimes he failed to get erections. But when he left them after this happened, he would not feel ignominious, he would feel justified: for who would want to sleep with an unattractive prostitute? These encounters were simply a way for him to express being alive in spite of feeling guilt and shame about what they were doing to him and what he was paying them for.

For that was the trouble; he did feel half-dead most of the time. In fact, life and death had become a subject he pondered a lot, his own death notwithstanding. He had lost all desire to live a long time and had developed a devil-may-care attitude to most things apart from his work in which he buried his head. This was why he had joined a climbing club and had been taking flying lessons at Cambridge Airport. He had a longing to be able to take a small plane up into the sky alone and to have his own life in his own hands and be in a position where it would be easy to choose.

A couple of days before they left for Wales, Mike said, 'I hope that woman is making her own way there. I don't really fancy the journey with three people, two dogs and all the gear.'

Even now, though he was sure he had fallen out of love, he felt the same old stab of jealousy about Bette choosing to be with someone else. Just as he now called Bette 'my partner', he dissociated himself from this Christmas guest.

'That woman, as you choose to call her, is bringing her own car... if it makes it.'

'What d'you mean?'

'It's a bit old and dilapidated. Besides, we'll need two cars. We'll want to do different things some of the time.'

Thank God, he thought. And *most* of the time, he hoped.

'She's got her walking gear with her and the dog's bed.'

'You could have just invited her for Christmas instead of a fortnight. We'll get no alone time together and I shall feel like such a gooseberry.' He was lying through his teeth, but he knew he had still to make some effort to let Bette think he loved her. He was a conflicted man, for underneath he knew he still did really. It was just so difficult to know how to get the relationship back on track. He was pretty sure they both felt the same way but he simply couldn't find the way to get it there. Their mutual sadness meant that so much distance had come between them. So much of the time they had to force smiles, force politeness, force tolerance of one another.

He wondered whether she blamed him. His heart told him she should. In fact, she quite often gave him the impression that she did. It never occurred to him to attach any blame to Bette whatsoever.

In a short time, Bette had become a part of his life. It may not have been obvious, as most people thought of her as a gregarious person, but she was actually not at all. In fact, she was quite a mystery; full of contradictions. She liked quiet, she liked long, silent walks, she liked reading, drawing, design and art but not particularly going out. Of course, she had made a few Cambridge acquaintances but she had no intention of joining in local activities and was probably considered stuck-up. But Mike knew she wasn't really. It was simply that she was not someone people found easy to stay friends with. Although ebullient, her outspokenness and sometimes slightly false 'life of the party' air she put on, scared most females away. Mike thought Bette probably presented a threat to other women, the way she so enjoyed male attention.

For a moment, Mike felt the old warmth he used to feel when he thought about her and he was glad she had at last made a proper friend.

He watched her. She seemed to have a little spring in her step as she started bustling about writing lists for Christmas Day and what they would need to take. *We should have gone up there before,* he thought, and felt a real sense of failure as a partner. He had not been looking after her. He had only thought of himself and his own grief, not of her and hers. *Poor little Bette,* he thought, *I really will make more effort to put her first and help her get some enjoyment back.*

He started thinking about the drive there. It was a good five and a half hours and they must allow a lunch stop where Brynn could have a pee and they could grab something to eat and drink.

By the end of that day, both Bette and Mike felt lighter than they had for a long time.

Bette called Mrs Edwards and asked her to pop into Cliff Edge on the morning of the twenty-third to get the wood burner going, turn the heating up and generally tidy the place and make up the beds.

15

23–24 DECEMBER 2017. CLIFF EDGE

Sara had a satnav and had been invited to arrive on Christmas Eve. Mike and Bette wanted a night there alone to get the house heated up and some shopping in before their guest arrived.

It was little short of 300 miles to Cliff Edge from Cambridge and Bette and Mike left soon after 9 o'clock in the morning, intending to go via Bristol and the Severn Bridge.

Because Mike was silent on the journey, Bette presumed he was in a huff and was wishing he hadn't agreed to the idea. He could sulk like a child when things didn't go his way. She usually dealt with it by giving him the silent treatment in return. In the game of silence, she could easily outlast him and it would always be him to apologise just to get her to talk to him again. She had once kept it up for ten days.

In the car, Bette turned on the stereo and switched from Mike's jazz-and-blues playlist to a radio station playing relentless Christmas pop songs. She sang along loudly and slightly out of tune to Mariah Carey, Slade and others until Mike could bear it no more. He was certain she had done it deliberately to annoy. Silently, he altered the stereo back to his beloved jazz.

An angry glare from Bette accompanied words spat rather than spoken. 'Eat your heart out, Scrooge,' she addressed the air. 'This year Michael Hanson takes the crown. Enjoyment's a thing he refuses to try and understand and since I gave up trying to enjoy him years ago, this Christmas I fully intend to enjoy me, moi, my little old self. He will not get me down this Christmas, of that he can be certain.'

Mike fiddled with the settings until he found the station she had been listening to. He couldn't face the rest of the drive in a bitter atmosphere and took the line of least resistance.

Without a word, Bette joined in the chorus of another Christmas song and no more was said about it.

They made better progress than expected and it was about ten minutes before two when they stopped near the Severn for a bite in the pub and to let the dog stretch his legs. They were glad they'd brought their padded coats and thermal underwear as it was forecast to be a cold Christmas. It wasn't so bad in the valleys, but up on the hills and beside the coast, it could be a different story. A high wind was getting up. It was certainly going to freeze that evening. Cliff Edge would be warm, though, as they'd asked Mrs Edwards to leave it on a time switch since the beginning of November when four people had visited it. They'd learned that lesson last Christmas, when Bette had been eight months pregnant. The place had been freezing when they arrived and had taken quite a while to warm up.

They branched off the motorway to stop at a pub in the countryside for a late lunch and to allow Brynn to have a run and a pee. Mike ordered a lager and a lamb steak and she her beloved curry, rice and chips. The mood was brightening up and Mike was speaking again.

She was hardly listening. It wasn't as though she cared whether he spoke or not. He leant across the table and for the first time in ages, fixed her with that intense look of his. 'I know

I've been a total grump since... well, you know... and I'm very sorry and I'm going to try to look on the brighter side starting now and in the new year.'

'Don't bother about it,' said Bette.

'I've been wondering. What would you say to trying again?'

'What do you mean?'

'At having a baby.'

'Have you lost your mind?' Bette was crying. 'I cannot believe my ears. How can you even suggest such a thing? It would be like trying to stick the most useless little plaster over a huge wound. The answer is no!' Her voice was high and loud and people at other tables stopped eating and turned to look at her.

He sank back into his seat. Her words chastised and hurt deeply but then he told himself, he had tried the idea too soon. In fact, it was still raw and probably *was* too soon. Perhaps if he could get back his old positivity... He would wait until next year then work on her again. He apologised for distressing her but inside, his anger was rising against her and against himself for not standing up to her, for not making her see that another baby was the answer.

This contained resentment had been with him ever since Lucy's death and showed no signs of dissipating. In fact, for every day that went by, it quietly grew.

Before reaching Cliff Edge, they stopped again in Newport to grab milk, butter and bread for breakfast the next day. On a whim, Bette bought a Christmas tree so large that they had to strap it to the roof. This irritated Mike hugely who tried to stop her and said it was ridiculous to buy one now as it could have waited till tomorrow when they did the big shop. But Bette got furious and stamped her foot and yelled at him in front of the guy who was helping carry the tree to the car. Once they had managed to secure the thing to the car, Mike could barely see out to drive the rest of the way and angrily steered slowly along toward the cliff road to their house. A pall of mashed-up feelings hung in the air between them but both of them knew Bette had got her way – for now.

She had bought an expensive frozen fish pie and some broccoli for supper and so they were set up until the following morning when they'd go shopping. They kept a large plastic box with larder products such as coffee, tea, salt, and sugar in the garden shed so they didn't need to keep replacing them every time they went. They also kept a case of wine and a crate of beer in there. The locals were all honest, good people and they weren't worried that anyone would steal anything. Besides, it was widely known that the house was rented out.

They drove down the quarter-mile track to Cliff Edge and parked the car. It felt strange to be back at a place where they had shared happiness. As they got out of the car, Bette wished she hadn't suggested coming here for Christmas.

First of all, they had to drag the cumbersome Christmas tree off the roof rack. Then they took their luggage into the house. The place was immaculate. Mrs Edwards had clearly been in, got the heating going, lit the wood burner and stacked a few logs ready. Bette fed Brynn then sent the disgruntled Mike out to the shed to fetch the box with their provisions and the Christmas tree holder (she'd put it away in there last year). When he returned, Bette positioned the holder and then they went to stagger into the house with the tree which dropped pine needles all over the clean floor.

Mike, who just wanted to sit down and have a glass of wine and something to eat, was becoming more irritated by the second. Once the tree was up, Bette put the fish pie in the oven and poured both of them a glass of wine. They sat by the wood burner but talk stuck in their mouths. Then she remembered. Sara was coming tomorrow. That should make things a lot more fun.

That evening while they barely spoke, Bette decorated the tree with baubles and tinsel. In spite of the atmosphere, she was beginning to really look forward to Christmas.

The following morning at first light Bette slipped out and cut some Christmas greenery. Later, before they set off for the market in Fishguard, Mike took Brynn for a short run, and Bette made a centrepiece of holly and ivy for the table.

While she was busy at this a loud thud echoed through the house. The heavy, old iron door knocker Mike had found in an antique shop could make a big noise. Bette answered the door to find the tiny, kind-faced Mrs Edwards smiling cheerily with a bag in her hand. 'I've bought you a little something to wish you a very merry Christmas. Nice to have you back.'

Bette gushed over her home-made teacakes and laverbread. In return, she told her she had put a hundred pounds bonus into her account that day. Showing gratitude was not a thing Mrs Edwards had been brought up to do. The nearest thing to it that she could manage was to say, 'That'll come in nice and handy.'

Her husband had drowned when his trawler had sunk in Carmarthen Bay some ten years before and Mrs Edwards had been left to bring up her only child. He was now grown and lived in Swansea so she didn't see him much. Along with making and selling Welsh teacakes and collecting seaweed to cook for hours to make the laverbread that she also sold, the spasmodic work at Cliff Edge helped her manage.

She was about to leave when Mike reappeared and, always the gentleman, insisted on driving her back to her cottage. It was only a couple of miles but in the cold weather and with the icy roads, Mrs Edwards, who had bicycled up to Cliff Edge, demurred with little show of resistance. While Mike lifted and secured her bike onto his roof rack, she said she was going to her son's the following day for Christmas and the new year but that she'd be back on the 2nd January and would come up to give the place a good clean that afternoon.

Mike and Bette now drove to the market in Fishguard where they stocked up with all kinds of delicious food including pre-ordered beef, ham, crab, lobsters, cheeses, and cakes.

By the afternoon, the burner crackling, mince pies cooking in the oven, Mike went out again to take Brynn out for half an hour before darkness started to fall. Five minutes after he left, a car sounded outside. Bette ran out to greet Sara. She got out of the car and let Gin out of the boot. The women hugged one another.

Sara's delight in the place was immediately obvious. 'Oh my God, Bette, what an amazing building and in such a stunning setting.' They watched Gin run around sniffing Brynn's trail, her carefully-groomed tricolour coat blowing wild in the wind.

Sara removed Gin's fleece bed and her case from the car.

'Oh Bette, this place is just wonderful. This is going to be my best Christmas ever. But where's the gorgeous Brynn?'

'Mike and Brynn are walking. They won't be long then the dogs can go crazy together. It's so remote here, we just leave Brynn to his own devices a lot of the time. Put those cases down now. I want to quickly show you the outside.'

Sara dropped the case and fleece as bidden while Bette took her round the garden, pointing out the cliffs and the rough sea beyond. 'You're probably dying for the toilet and a cup of tea though not necessarily in that order, but I just had to show you the landscape.'

They went inside and Sara swooned with over-the-top pleasure and straightaway wanted to explore. 'Oh Bette, it's more wonderful than I can believe. What a place! And you've done it so beautifully. It's quite awe-inspiring. The people who lived here long ago would applaud how you have rescued and turned it into such a beautiful home. But you were right about the toilet. Badly needed.'

Bette showed her the cloakroom while she made a pot of tea. When Sara came back into the kitchen, Bette said, 'Not bad, is it? Blowy at this time of year but that's what you get so close to the sea. It makes up for it in the summer: there's wonderful watching – boats, seabirds, seals, dolphins, porpoises and sometimes we get basking sharks.' She picked up Sara's tatty case. 'I'll show you your bedroom.'

'Don't you dare– I mean, don't take my case.' Her usual ingratiating self.

Bette took the case anyway while Sara carried the dog bed.

'Where should Gin sleep?'

'Wherever you like, it really doesn't matter.'

'Well, er, if it's okay she is used to sleeping on the floor beside my bed. She feels more relaxed when she's with me. Would that be okay?'

'Of course, no problem. Brynn actually sneaks in with me when Mike's away but he's such a clean-freak he doesn't like the idea of a dog in the bedroom. Silly man.'

So he was called Mike. The name was not spoken with love but at least the man had one.

'Oh, I'm sure most people don't. But thank you, as long as you're sure it won't annoy Mike?'

'I'll deal with him if it does,' Bette said quickly. 'He shouldn't be long, I told him to be back by 4pm.'

Surprised at the vehemence with which she spoke of her partner, Sara thought Bette must be in a mood. She had previously witnessed how it could change. Fortunately, this seldom lasted and Bette, who was by and large a happy person, forgot any ill temper quickly.

They climbed the iron staircase and walked along the gallery to the pale-blue bedroom with which Sara was delighted.

Through one of the original windows, a view of wintery grass fields stretched to the coastal path along the cliffs, beyond which a grey, choppy sea frothed and crashed against the rockface.

'What they call bracing weather,' said Bette. 'The forecast says there's snow on the way next week.'

'Quite a change from Cambridge. It's not so cold down there.' Sara hugged her. 'Oh Bette, I am so happy to be here.'

What Bette would term sycophantic most would say was exaggerated politeness.

'And we are *so* pleased you've come. You get yourself unpacked and settled then join us downstairs. Mike is dying to meet you.'

At about quarter past four in the afternoon, Bette was standing reading a cookery book in the kitchen area and Mike was sitting on the big sofa, reading the newspaper. Sara came down the iron staircase, a happy grin on her face. As she reached the penultimate step from the floor, she stopped dead. For a few moments, she looked as though she might be going to faint. Bette, who hadn't noticed, called to Mike, 'Sara's here. Come and say hello.'

Mike glanced up. He hesitated before leaving his chair and on his way across the room paused to put a couple of logs in the wood burner before walking toward Sara. He shook her hand. 'Hello. Glad you made it.'

Sara stammered a greeting then murmured that she had forgotten something and would they excuse her, please.

'Are you all right?' Bette stared at her.

Sara looked as though she was about to burst into tears. 'No, no, I mean, yes, no, everything's fine. I'm– I'm just a bit exhausted after the journey. Would you mind terribly if I had a lie down in my bedroom? I've got one of my migraines coming on and am not feeling very well.'

'Has something happened, Sara? Tell me.'

'No, no, I just... I just... I'm getting one of my migraines. I'm so sorry, I must go to bed.' She ran back up the stairs.

Bette looked at Mike. 'Whatever do you think is wrong with her?'

'No idea.' Mike took a mince pie and bit into it.

'S'posed to have cream with it, you dimp.'

He appeared not to hear her as he returned to his paper.

Bette fished around in the fridge, found some root ginger, chopped a chunk up into tiny pieces and took it upstairs to find Sara sitting on the bed holding her head in her hands and crying.

'Oh Sara, I'm worried about you. Whatever's troubling you, you can tell me, you know. We've shared our deepest secrets already. Tell me what it is. Is it something about this place?'

'No, of course not. No really, it's this awful head. I actually felt it coming on as I was arriving. I've told you about them before. I do get these attacks, you know. The long drive probably brought it on. I just need to sleep. I'll hopefully be fine by the morning.' Her eyes were still watery and she was pale.

'Poor you. I've brought some ibuprofen, water and chopped-up ginger to put on your forehead. You probably already know it's a brilliant recipe for getting rid of headaches. Now then, you get undressed, get into bed and I'll do it for you.' She put the glass of water on the bedside table. Sara got up to move toward her still-unpacked suitcase. Bette was being wonderful. Like the best nurse.

'Hey, I'll do that for you. You stay there.'

Before Sara could stop her, Bette had unzipped her suitcase and was going through her things. 'Ah, there we are, what a pretty pair of PJs and warm too. Just what's needed in this weather.' She held up the faded mauve pyjamas that had clearly seen better days before handing them to Sara who blushed and tried to put them on without exposing her body to Bette.

'Oh, don't be concerned on my behalf, lovely, I've seen it all.'

As Sara got into bed, Bette handed her two tablets and the glass. Once she had swallowed them and was lying under the duvet, Bette scattered the tiny pieces of ginger on her forehead. After a short time, Sara began to feel the heat from the root.

'Leave it on until it gets too hot to bear.' Bette crossed to the door. 'I'll pop up later to see if you'd like some soup or something easy for a light supper. We have to have you better for Christmas, you know.'

She blew a kiss to Sara. 'Rest and get better, darling. I'll pop up later.'

At around 8pm, Bette crept upstairs as quietly as possible and peeped into Sara's room. Gin was lying at the bottom of the bed and Sara sitting up with her knees bent up under the bedclothes, her laptop balanced on them. She snapped the machine shut.

'Hey! You shouldn't be looking at that.' Bette was annoyed. 'Screens are notoriously bad for headaches.' She moved to the bedside, picked up the laptop, crossed the room and put it on the dressing table. 'Trying to get on the internet? I'll give you the password tomorrow. There's plenty of time for that. I honestly don't think you should look at that this evening. Now then, here's a couple more ibuprofen. The head seems to be better which is great news. That ginger trick is brilliant, isn't it? Come down and join us for some supper. It's only soup and cheese. We're holding back for tomorrow's feast.'

Sara said quickly, 'Bette, my head is slightly better but I'd rather spend the evening up here if that's okay with you. Moving around can stir it up again. I want to be okay for tomorrow.'

'Oh, all right then.' Bette was clearly miffed. 'Such a shame, especially as you've driven all this way and it's Christmas Eve. Still, if that's how you feel...' She sat down on the bed and leant towards Sara. In a confidential tone she asked, 'This may sound odd but I wondered if the headache had something to do with meeting Mike. You seemed fine until then.'

Exasperated, Sara answered her. 'Of *course* not. What an *absurd* question, Bette.'

'If you say so. I just wondered whether your bad experience meant you find dealing with any man tricky.'

'No, no. Honestly, it was the drive that caused the headache. One hundred per cent. It's hard for people who don't experience migraines to understand them. They are not headaches. Much, much worse.'

'Okay, okay, if you say so.'

The hint was in the words and the tone that Bette didn't believe her. Sara wondered why she didn't accept her word. A contest was starting.

'I'll bring you up a bowl of beef consommé, very good for invalids. Won't be long.'

Sara was about to remind Bette that she wasn't a meat eater but Bette shut the door rather louder than necessary.

Beef! Had she really forgotten that Sara avoided red meat? She had already discovered that Bette was not a woman to be thwarted. But then, Sara reminded herself, neither was she.

24 December 2017. Bette Davies' Five-Year Diary
How I wish it were this time last year when little Lucy was nestling inside me and we were still so happy here. But I must try to carry on and make the best of it. Sara's here so that should be fun. Wish Mike would cheer up a bit. He's so angry all the time. Perhaps he will tomorrow. It's Christmas!

16

25 DECEMBER 2017. CLIFF EDGE

B ette yawned. She glanced at her watch. It was 7.42am and it was Christmas Day. The past few Christmases had been the happiest she had ever had. Her parents had been far too stingy even to get a turkey. She remembered that New Year's Eve when she and Mike had had the first of what had gone on to be many nights of wonderful sex. And now, here they were, a miserable three stuck in the middle of nowhere. Mike was either still asleep or pretending to be. That's what they both did a lot nowadays.

She got out of bed, showered in their en-suite bathroom, dried herself, threw on a thick towelling robe, slipped her feet into a pair of furry slippers and went downstairs.

Brynn greeted her with his usual enthusiasm and as she bent down to give him a *cwtch* while he licked her face, she thought he was the only good thing in her life and she thanked an invisible God (that she had absolutely no faith or belief in) for bringing him to her.

She went upstairs with a mug of tea and a packet of paracetamol and down the balcony to Sara's room. She quietly opened the door and popped her head round it.

'Oh, you're awake. Oh great. You must be feeling better. Ginger helped, did it? I'm so glad. Brought you a cup of tea. Happy Christmas!'

Sara swore she had said coffee when Bette had asked her the previous evening whether she preferred that or tea in the mornings. *But hey,* she thought, *who am I to grumble when my kind friend is taking such good care of me?*

Bette went back to her bedroom. She sat on the bed. She smiled. She was enjoying herself for the first time for a while. 'Happy Christmas, Mike. Your present is under the tree. But we're opening them later.'

He stretched his long body, sat up and checked his watch. 'Happy Christmas,' he said and for the first time in ages leant forward to give Bette a quick kiss on the lips. 'Yours is, too.'

'Sara seems to be better so I'm happy to say she'll be joining us. Apparently, she gets migraines quite a lot. But then I suppose it's not surprising when you consider what she's been through this year.'

Mike got out of bed and wandered towards the bathroom. 'What's that's then?'

Leaning on the bathroom door frame, Bette told her partner Sara's story about the lover and the miscarriage that had followed.

Then Bette piled her thick blonde hair up on top of her head, a look she knew Mike loved, and put on a tight red dress over navy leggings tucked into red, pointed, stiletto ankle boots and went downstairs to make breakfast.

As Sara came downstairs the smell of cooking bacon wafted toward her and she felt mildly nauseous. Bette was swaying along to a Christmas playlist coming from a smart speaker as she cooked. She waved to Sara to come and sit down.

Sara had pulled on a beige jumper and a pair of black trousers and the moment she saw how glamorous Bette looked she wished she'd dressed up a bit more. After all, she had packed the blue sequin blouse and the blue high heels but had not felt it would be fitting to wear them, having had such a bad start to her stay.

'How many bits of bacon do you want?' asked Bette.

'Oh...' said Sara awkwardly. 'I don't... I don't feel up to bacon. So just eggs for me.'

Bette banged a plate of eggs and some sort of green mush down on the table before Sara. Sara did not like to ask about the mush, but she tasted it and then forced it down. The atmosphere grew tense before Mike joined them a while later.

Mike seemed edgy and glum, and spoke little, except to ask for more laverbread.

So that's what the green mush is, thought Sara.

'Cheer up, you lot. It's Christmas.' Bette turned up the volume so that festive pop songs filled Cliff Edge's high rafters. Her ebullience was at odds with the mood and demonstrated that if no one else was, she was clearly enjoying herself.

Mike wiped his mouth with his napkin, pushed the finished plate forward and left the table. 'I plan on a long walk. Is it okay to leave the washing-up to you? I must chop up some more wood later.'

'You seem out of sorts, darling. What's up? You feeling all right?'

'I'm fine. Just a bit of a tummy.'

'Oh, you poor love. Should you go out? Why not stay here and let me care for you.'

'No, I think a walk will help settle it.'

'Okay then, if you're sure. No problem, us girls can cope.

Snow's forecast to hit us sometime during the next forty-eight hours, you know.'

But that didn't put him off. He put on his big brown parka, his beanie and gloves, took his trekking poles and left Cliff Edge, Brynn at his side. A cold blast hit her as Bette opened the door and called after him, 'What about Gin? Wont you take her with you?'

He stopped walking, looked back, clearly exasperated. 'But I don't know the dog... I didn't know if it would want to come with me.'

'Oh yes, she'd love it – she's great friends with Brynn and will stick near him.'

But when Bette called Gin to her, Sara looked worried.

'I'm really not sure Gin will be happy to go.'

'She'll be fine. You must stop worrying, Sara. You fret too much. It's Christmas. Relax and enjoy yourself.'

When Bette reopened the front door again, Mike had already set off.

'Hey! Wait!' she shouted. 'Call Gin, Mike.'

As so often he did, Mike complied with Bette's instruction and whistled to the dog who ran to join Brynn where they immediately romped in the frosted field.

'Lunch at 1.30!' she shouted after him. He didn't reply but she presumed he'd heard her. She watched him walk over the field down toward the coastal path.

'Help me prep lunch, sweetie? No turkey, I'm afraid. We'd be eating it for weeks afterwards. Instead I got a fillet of beef and it'll be Yorkshire puddings, gratin potatoes, brussels sprouts, carrots, celeriac puree, roast chestnuts and then we've got a traditional Christmas pudding with my home-made brandy butter which doesn't skimp on the brandy.' Bette flashed her most attractive smile. 'Not too over the top, is it?'

Her ironic tone spoke volumes. In spite of the beef, Sara shook her head and laughed.

'No, not at all. Sounds lovely.'

'It's going to be a real blockbuster meal. No walks for us today, just eating, boozing, flopping and watching television. That's what Christmas should be, don't you think?'

What Bette had described was what Sara's parents and many people in her hometown would have called gluttony, wickedness and idleness. Sara was torn about how to feel. Although she approved of and wanted to share Bette's enjoyment of good things, she also had a deeply instilled puritanical streak that told her it was wrong. But she said, 'I certainly do.'

'Time for some champagne.' That Bette was in celebratory mood was clear.

'Shouldn't we wait for er... Mike to get back?'

'No, he can have some later.' She took a bottle out of the fridge and fetched two champagne flutes from a cupboard. 'I for one, intend to start the day as I mean to go on.'

When she had heard what was for lunch today, Sara told herself she must simply get on with it. It was Christmas and why, on her behalf, should her hosts eat anything they would not normally have had on that day. Bette had been so kind to her and had no idea how deeply disturbed she was feeling or why.

But she couldn't help thinking back to her dour childhood Christmases where the family spent most of the day in church or at prayer. As she cut the celeriac in half and peeled the tough skin away, she realised one of the big differences between herself and her friend was that if she felt something, she was unlikely to voice it whereas Bette would say what she thought.

While Bette studied a cookbook and prepared thin slices of potato for a gratin dauphinoise and Sara chopped the peeled celeriac into chunks, the deep-seated, usually well-hidden jealousy of Bette surfaced and gnawed at Sara's mind. She gripped the fierce chopping knife.

In the darkest depths of her being she felt a long-forgotten urge rise in her that had to be repressed. As she threw the pieces into water to boil, she added a large amount of salt. Whether she had done so deliberately or not, she was not certain. But she knew the puree Bette was so keen on having would taste very far from the delicious accompaniment she imagined.

Venom in her heart, she cut the tops off the brussels sprouts while Bette poured double cream and then hot milk over the sliced potatoes, garlic and nutmeg before going on to make the Yorkshire pudding mix and prepare the carrots ready for roasting around the joint in the oven.

'I won't put the beef in until the master returns. It should only take about half an hour as we love it pink and rare – oops! Sorry – I should have asked before – hope you like it that way? Rare, I mean, but if you don't, we'll make sure you get the outer slices, they'll be the best done.'

Sara's stomach heaved at the thought of the bleeding red meat she would not only have to see but force down. She contemplated reminding Bette that she wasn't a red meat eater. She wanted to be bold and say she'd rather not have any but she was determined not to give Bette any more ammo against her since her hostess had seemed so annoyed with her the previous evening.

She would be even more upset if she knew that the beef consommé had gone down the bathroom sink, Sara thought, a touch of satisfaction in her churning brain. All she had eaten the previous evening had been the hunks of bread Bette had brought up with it. She also knew that if she refused the meat, that oh-so familiar guilt would rise up and permeate her being. In the complexity that was Sara, her desires clashed with a forcibly imbued idea of morality.

But when having refused a second glass of champagne, Sara watched Bette's enjoyment as she quaffed her own second glass, then she changed her mind and decided that today she would wave those inhibitions out of the window.

'On second thoughts... I should love another, please.'

'That's the spirit, darling.' Bette refilled Sara's glass.

They chinked glasses and Bette laid the table for lunch, putting jolly red napkins and home-made black Christmas crackers with tiny red nametags around each place setting.

'Looks lovely. Well done, Bette.' Sara struggled to suppress vile thoughts.

Mike returned a bit later than Bette had said and she rushed the beef into the oven as she heard the front door open. In half an hour, she was serving up the lunch.

'Carve, would you.' No mistaking this command as a question.

'Of course. This looks like a delicious lunch. Sorry I haven't been here to help.'

'You're not, but you should be,' Bette snapped. 'We worked hard enough, didn't we, Sara?'

Embarrassed by Bette's rudeness, Sara mumbled, 'Well, it wasn't too hard really.' She had gone quieter than ever now the man was around again.

Before they sat down at the table, Bette produced her iPhone, inviting them to pose in front of it. They both stood awkwardly beside one another. 'Hey, come on you two, smile. Mike, put an arm round Sara. I want some happy Christmas pics.' She snapped a few then moved to stand next to Sara where she took a few selfies of their three faces. The others managed strained grins while she gave her flashiest, whitest smile.

Sara thought she should reciprocate and try at least to look as though she was enjoying herself so she snapped some photos of the table and Bette and Mike with the dogs around whose necks Bette had tied red bows.

The salty celeriac puree that had been Sara's contribution almost spoilt the main course. They each had a taste. Highly irritated, Bette pulled a face and said, 'The puree's far too salty. I suggest we leave it. Never mind, Sara, you tried your best.'

The implication was not lost on Sara who was quietly pleased her plan had worked but seethed at Bette's suggestion that her best was so poor.

The salt wasn't the only taste in their mouths. Conversation was stilted and most of the talking was done by Bette who continued to present a cheerful front, drinking quite a bit as she went. But then they all were. Mike knocked back more red wine than he usually did and Sara, a generally moderate drinker, was well on her way to becoming drunk.

Bette produced a dessert wine from the fridge to go with the brandy-spiked Christmas pudding, with which they ate brandy butter. They just about managed to eat this before sitting back in their chairs almost unable to move for being so satiated.

Unused as she was to indulging her appetite to such a degree, Sara had by now thrown all her cares away. She had not drunk so much alcohol in years but was now experiencing a mixture of elation and confusion, both of which helped her through what she would have considered the most gluttonous, stressful meal of her life.

Bette poured everyone another glass of the delicious French, sweet white wine.

'Time for the crackers.' She looked as excited as a kid. 'You each have your own. I made them myself. Pretty aren't they?' The others murmured their approval. 'Ladies first. Here's yours, Sara.'

Hesitantly, Sara attempted to pull the unpromising black cracker with both hands but unable to manage, Bette took one end and they pulled it apart together. It snapped with a bang and out fell a woman's pink thong and a Father Christmas hat.

'See what it reads on your thong then.' Bette was insistent. Sara stretched the front triangular piece of pink fabric out to find black text that read:

ALL I WANT FOR CHRISTMAS IS
SEX
(WITH ANYONE).

Normally, she would have been mortified with embarrassment, but now Sara barked with laughter. She put the hat on and the thong over her trousers and walked about giggling and swaying her hips in an unlikely provocative fashion. Disconcerted by Sara's gift and more so her behaviour, Mike couldn't watch her.

'Go on, Mike, your turn.' The red-faced man snapped his cracker. It contained a Father Christmas hat and a strange little black cotton bag with a thin elastic strap attached. In red text a caption on the black piece read, 'DYING FOR IT'.

'What the hell is this?'

'A posing pouch. You pop your meat and two veg in it – like a thong for men.'

Bette and Sara cackled with drunken laughter while Mike could not contain his anger. Red with wine and annoyance, he jumped to his feet and threw the thong on the floor. 'What kind of a joke do you call that?' he bellowed.

'Oh darling, really. Why are you taking it so badly? I'm so sorry if I've upset you. I thought you would laugh about it.'

Bette looked downcast and stopped laughing while Mike's fury turned to awkward humiliation. He mumbled something of an apology before sitting down at the table again. Then, thinking better of it, unexpectedly leapt to his feet again. He slammed a fist down on the table. 'Actually, you've gone too far, Bette. I don't know what you were thinking giving us such ridiculous, childish, dirty-minded gifts.'

Bette was now clearly remorseful. Like a ticked-off kid she hung her head in shame before lifting it up again and looking Mike directly in the eyes. 'I didn't leave myself out, you know. Look what I've got.' She tore open her own cracker. She glanced up at Mike. 'I'm only trying to have a bit of fun, mun.'

On the table lay a flimsy red bikini. Bette held it over her chest. Over the right breast a message in black read DROP, on the other, DEAD and on the bottom half, GORGEOUS.

Now Mike felt bad. So did Sara who got up and hugged her poor pal who, after all, had had a horrible year and was only trying to enjoy life again. Besides, if it did rub up Mike's sensibilities, all the better as far as she was concerned. After all, Bette didn't mean anything by it.

To her surprise, as quickly as Bette's spirits had crashed, they had risen again. She jumped up. Sara started to clear away the table but Bette caught hold of her arm.

'No, no, sweetness, thanks but that comes later.' In a comic-dramatic gesture, she pointed across the room. 'Now, lady and gentleman,' she said in an exaggerated announcer's voice, 'I give you... the tree.'

She wove her way past the wood burner to the other end of the room where her Christmas tree stood in the centre of the glass doors. In a stagey manner, she closed the long pale-grey linen curtains behind it, walked back round, swaying as she went in archly sexual fashion and stood hand on one hip in a provocative pose in front of the tree. The others were still at the table wordlessly watching her.

'Come on, you two, no time like the present. Get it?' She

rocked with laughter again. 'Bring your drinks, darlings, and come and sit over here.'

And like obedient children they did as they were told, each sitting on one of the large sofas either side of the tree.

'That's not very friendly. Go on, sit on the same side. Get up and join Sara, Mike.'

He rose and walked stiffly across to the other sofa. Bette bent down, an overtly sexual tilt to her bottom and picked up a gold envelope under the tree with 'Sara' on it.

'Sara, darling, happy Christmas, from Mike and me.' She crossed to her and handed her the envelope. There was a card enclosing a note explaining that twenty thousand pounds had been transferred into Sara's bank. The note went on to read:

I know times have been hard for you lately and this should help you get straight again. Please say NOTHING to Mike and don't give anything away!

Put this note straight back in the envelope and throw it away in the wood burner later.

The enclosed gold card you can show as your present!

Sara swallowed back a cry of disbelief. She could barely contain her amazement and sat for a good minute before it sank in. Prompted by Bette, she removed the gold postcard that was also inside.

Happy Christmas Sara! Congratulations and welcome to Perfect Stranger, the online dating website for finding the love of your life. Your profile is now complete.
You are a fully subscribed member from 24.12.2017 for one year until 24.12.2018.
Your username: Snow White!
Your password: Happilyeverafter?

She pocketed the envelope with the note and unable to cover her delight, gave Bette an extra-long hug and kissed her multiple times on the cheeks. Then she showed the dating website card to Mike, who now seemed even crosser. *Why would she be so thrilled about that?*

Bette then picked up a present from Mike to her. She opened it with a flourish to find a black silk and lace négligée from an expensive London boutique. She held it up in front of her and performed a mock belly dance. In a bitingly sarcastic tone she exclaimed, 'Oh my darling, what a wonderful present. I'll wear it tonight. That'll give you something to wank over.'

Sara looked shocked and Mike mortified. Bette then handed Mike his present carefully wrapped in black with a red bow. Opening it tentatively, he revealed a large silver-framed photograph of Lucy. He burst into tears.

Seemingly too drunk to notice, Bette wobbled over to sit down on the other side of Sara and cuddled her. 'Hope you like your pressie, darling?'

Sara was upset by Mike's reaction and struggled to show her gratitude. 'It's just what the doctor failed to order. I cannot thank you enough. What a truly wonderful friend you are, Bette.'

'Go on, you haven't opened mine to you, yet. I'm afraid it doesn't even begin to compete with yours.' Sara pointed to a present under the tree. 'And there's one for Mike, too. And one for you both.'

Nearly falling over her stilettos on the way, Bette staggered across to the tree and picked them up. She wobbled over to Mike who was trying to restore his equilibrium but failing.

'I feel too upset to open it at the moment. I'll do it later.' He turned to Sara. 'Thank you. Thank you so much.' As he got up from the sofa, he pecked her on the cheek. 'I need to go and lie down for a while. Too much wine.' He stood up and still sniffing back the tears, went upstairs to their bedroom. Sara put out a sympathetic hand and touched his arm as he got up to leave.

'That was going a bit far, wasn't it, Bette? Surely you knew it would upset him?'

'I thought he'd love it.' The cold tone was back in her voice. She tore the gold wrapping paper off the present to them both. It was another photo frame.

'Nice one, not sure what we'll put in it, but thanks, Sara.' Then she opened her present, also in gold paper. It was a hardback book written by a well-known celebrity who had lost a child to cot death and had then had another healthy baby who was then four years old.

In an explosion of rage, Bette leapt to her feet and screamed, 'How dare you? How fucking dare you? You fucking, stupid cunt!'

She stumbled across the room to drop the paper and the book into the wood burner. Multicoloured flames danced among the wrapping. 'Now who's being tactless? Huh? You think I want to read that shit? Do you? You moron.' Bette's rage did not unduly disturb Sara. It was nothing she hadn't expected.

'Oh dear, I feel awful, Bette, especially when you have given me such an incredibly generous gift.' She laid a conciliatory hand on her arm as Bette flung past her, grabbing and wrenching it away from her. Unthwarted, Sara continued, 'But I do think it's a shame. If you'd given it half a go you might have found that book inspiring and it might have helped you begin to get over what happened.'

'I don't *need* anyone's help. *Yours*,' Bette spat, 'least of all. I can very well "get over it" and look after myself.'

With that, she switched on the television, threw herself on the other sofa and watched with a bored, sulky expression.

Sara decided to leave her to it. She'd calm down in time. She left the living area, crossed to the kitchen-dining area of the huge room and quietly cleared away the lunch and loaded the dishwasher.

When she had finished, she said nothing, but went upstairs to her room, leaving Bette to simmer down.

Sara was torn. Earlier, she had wanted to punch Bette but had remembered that that was not the way forward. She had recalled the saying, *Don't get mad, get even*, and had known she must bide her time. But now, Bette had given her that huge sum of money and she had been dumbstruck by her generosity. What a strange cat the woman was. So unpredictable. So sweet and so sour. Now Sara must try to revise her thinking and the plan she had had in mind.

She lay on the bed experiencing an odd mixture of elation, fear and anger. She told herself her mind was playing tricks but she couldn't shake the feeling. Bette's behaviour that day had made her feel strangely alone. Like a fish out of water. But she reminded herself that sometimes she did feel like this and had read enough self-help books to know it was the result of being a runaway, a rootless person.

She wished so much she had just someone to rely on as a friend and had thought Bette was the one. But now... Too much whirred around her troubled mind. She went over the day in her mind. She had chosen the presents so carefully but Mike hadn't opened his. It would have hit just the spot and she was disappointed to miss seeing his face when he opened it.

With Bette, she had been prepared to expect a hostile reaction but not that the woman would feel quite so violently averse to the book.

By the time she tentatively emerged to come downstairs for supper, she was relieved to find Bette sound asleep and snoring on the sofa with Mike nowhere to be seen. Evidently still retired upstairs. His present would have to wait. There was always tomorrow. Tiptoeing quietly so as not to wake Bette, she made herself a couple of cheese sandwiches and a cup of tea, and gently whistling Gin who had followed her downstairs, fed the dog some leftover beef and vegetables.

Then she patted her leg to indicate Gin to follow and she crept back upstairs to her room. She climbed into bed, let Gin settle across her feet and sitting up ate her sandwiches and drank the tea. Then she put her laptop on her knees and searched the local area on the internet. She was particularly interested in the Witches' Cauldron.

17

26 DECEMBER 2017. CLIFF EDGE

On Boxing Day morning, Bette was up first, followed by Mike. Dreading seeing either of them, Sara avoided coming downstairs as long as she felt she could. Nursing the first hangover she had had since she had been in Amsterdam all that time ago, she felt queasy and dehydrated.

The couple sat in virtual silence at the breakfast table where Bette had laid cereals and put out some toast and marmalade. Mike looked miserable while she had resumed the cheerful demeanour she had had during yesterday's bizarre lunch.

Sara came downstairs at about 9.45 and kept her head lowered, avoiding eye contact with either of the couple.

But Bette, who for some reason didn't appear to have a hangover of her own, persuaded her to drink some cups of coffee and some orange juice and to eat a large bowl of muesli. And Sara began to feel human again. She thanked her friend for helping her feel that way.

'Oh, Mike, you still haven't yet opened your present from me.' She finished the last drops of coffee, jumped up enthusiastically from her chair and crossed the room to the Christmas tree where the present lay on the floor unopened. She picked it up and brought it back to the table.

Mike was eating some toast. His fourth piece, he was stocking up in readiness for his walk. He mumbled a thank you, delaying opening it until he had finished breakfast. When he had done so he tore the wrapping away to find a biography of Billie Holiday. He looked amazed.

Before he had a chance to say anything, Bette said, 'Are you psychic or something?'

'No, no, of course not. You told me Mike loved jazz and blues and especially Billie Holiday, don't you remember?'

'Did I?' Bette seemed vague. 'Don't remember doing so, that's for sure.'

'You did, Bette. Honestly you did, on one of our more recent walks. My memory is good.'

'Well, you couldn't have given me a better present, Sara.' Mike was still avoiding looking her in the eye as he thanked her.

'To be honest, when Bette said you loved Billie, I thought what good taste you must have and I would get you that book. But if you already have it, it can be changed at Waterstones in Cambridge.'

'No, it's new to me and will make riveting reading.' Mike seemed to have overcome his reluctance to engage and was now smiling openly at Sara and waving the book in the air. 'This will be pored over and scoured through and read more than once and, most of all, treasured, you can be sure. I am very grateful.'

He suddenly stood up and came around the table to where Sara was sitting. He put an arm round her shoulder and bent to kiss her on the cheek.

Clearly irritated by the empathy Mike was showing her friend, Bette abruptly scraped her chair back on the stone floor. Coldness edged her words. 'What are you doing today?'

'I was intending on walking westward on the cliff path this morning for a couple of hours but the wind may curtail that, depending how strong it blows. Shall I take the dogs with me?'

Sara said, 'Oh, that would be kind.'

'Sara will drive us in her car.' Bette was clearly irritated. 'I want to show her the views from Cilgerran Castle and after Pentre Ifan. We'll grab something to eat somewhere.'

'Okay. There's more than enough food to last for weeks here so I'll have something when I get back.'

'We may need it as snow is forecast either later today or tomorrow.'

Soon after breakfast, Mike dressed for a hike in harsh weather. Beanie pulled over his ears, gloves on, walking poles in hands, he whistled to the dogs who followed as he set off for the cliff path.

Having cleared away breakfast, the women donned their warmest clothes and got ready to go.

With Bette giving directions, Sara set off at the wheel. She felt uncomfortable about being alone with Bette after her outburst about the book she had given her, but apart from the earlier show of jealousy which Sara well understood, Bette appeared to be back on form today. They drove to Moylegrove then headed east as far as St Dogmaels before dropping south to bypass Cardigan and wind their way to Cilgerran.

'Glad we got rid of the man,' said Bette.

'Why are you so cross with him, Bette?'

'Because he has let me down.'

Sara knew she must tread warily here but she was dying to hear what Bette would say. 'In what way?'

'You really do love to ask questions, don't you?'

She could flare up again if she wasn't careful. But Sara persisted. 'In what way has he let you down?'

'He has not been a good partner to me. That's all you need to know. And by the way, I have no intention of ever having another child, thank you very much, so don't go giving me any more books about such things.' And Sara was shut down just like that.

A few small flakes of snow appeared from the sky. They flew about in the wind as though they didn't have the weight to land, or if they did land they melted instantly.

They drove on in silence for a while until Bette perked up and said, 'First, I'm taking you to see Cilgerran Castle. Thirteenth-century ruin. You'll like it. It's not far from here.'

Sara once again was flummoxed by Bette. She seemed to have changed since coming up to Wales. She was more extreme than in Cambridge. She wondered why that would be and looked for reasons. She remembered Bette's parents had both died in this county. It could be something to do with that, or maybe Cliff Edge reminded her of the happiness the couple had once so obviously shared. A happiness clearly gone now.

'Hang a right at the next turning.'

They parked and without speaking walked uphill to the castle, its two massive open towers looming above them. Being Boxing Day, it was officially closed by the National Trust but Bette was not to be outdone. She insisted Sara follow her as she scrambled dangerously around the edge of the river below where the castle was perched high over a gorge so close to the edge that parts of the outer walls had fallen to the valley below. Bette led them up a set of narrow, steep, spiral stone steps with a next-to-useless guard rail. Sara felt more than unsure about climbing up them.

'Bette, isn't this unsafe? I mean, I'm sure it's not when they're dry but the steps are quite slippery with the snow. We could meet our deaths going up here.'

'Oh, come on, you cackty. Just tread carefully. Where's Darer Sara gone? It'll be worth it, you'll see.'

'Cackty?' Sara's voice was trembling.

'Coward! But of course I'm not serious, darling, you're not really a cackty, just a little bit right now.'

'I'd call it sensible.' Sara managed to laugh. And the two women giggled as they gingerly picked their way up the stairs.

And Bette was right, it was indeed worth it. They had to climb over a railing at the top but once at the top there were some spectacular views. As they stood close to the edge, Sara said, 'Don't you wish you could go back in time and ask the builders of this magical place why they put so much effort into moving and hacking such huge stones. What fear was so great that motivated them?'

'Death, darling. Death.'

'Yes, well, I suppose... and building it probably killed quite a few of them.'

'They did as they were told, sweetie. If they didn't, they'd have died of starvation from lack of money.'

Sara was close to the guard rail at the top of the edge above the gorge. Bette walked up behind her. 'Careful there, darling, you don't want to join their ranks just yet, do you?'

'Oh, I'm definitely not ready to go yet. How about you, Bette?' Sara turned around to face her. Bette ignored Sara's question and changed the subject.

'The snow has already stopped. Not sure why it bothered.'

'I think they call it a flurry, don't they?'

'Who's they?' Bette said with a smirk.

All of a sudden, Sara leaned forward and put her arms round Bette's waist. She tried to kiss her on the lips, but Bette flinched away.

'No way, José,' she said. 'Not my bag, Sara. I thought you knew.'

Sara laughed it off. 'But, as you would say, darling, if at first you don't succeed, try, try, try again.'

She had backfooted Bette, for once. A new rivalry between them had taken seed. It might have been thought of as having to do with familiarity and contempt but in truth both women were highly competitive people. While Bette didn't care who knew it, Sara, being the more devious of the two, took care to hide the drive she had within. The same drive that had led her to desert her family.

They descended by the road and returned to the car a safer way.

'That was wonderful. Thank you, Bette.' This time, Sara decided she probably shouldn't hug her again. She told herself she must remember that in spite of how difficult Bette could be, she usually meant well. After all, there was no need for her to have brought her on this outing. Underneath her volatile nature, she was a kind person. Except that is, when it came to Mike. She had a heavy grudge against her partner and Sara longed to know what it was all about. She had tried before to drag it out of Bette with no luck. Maybe she'd get her to open up after a few drinks this evening.

It was getting on for noon when they headed for Pentre Ifan.

'More treats in store. If you liked the ancient history associated with the castle, wait till you see this place. It's amazing.'

A short drive and the women arrived at one of the most beautiful views in Wales. Sara was enthralled by the collection of megaliths, known as the Stonehenge of Wales.

'Oh God, Bette,' she said, staring up at the three great standing stones supporting a giant capstone, 'this is just extraordinary. I feel so insignificant beside this place. When was it built?'

'About four thousand years BC. Something, isn't it?' Both women gaped at the enormous stones.

'But how did they get such vast boulders here? And more so, how did they lift the stone on top? It must weigh tonnes.'

'I think it's fifteen tonnes or more. To this day, there are many theories but none are certain. I always come here when I'm at Cliff Edge. Reminds me what mankind is capable of. If they could do this then, what can we do now? Also, it reminds you you're mortal, doesn't it? It's a burial ground, supposedly.'

'Yes, I thought it might be. A thought-provoking place.'

'Contemplating your future again, Sara?'

'Our future, I would say.'

They walked around the perimeter of the stones in silence. The vast rocks seemed all the more beautiful for their icing of fine snow. They stood and gazed in awe for a time.

'Right. Lunch now in Newport's finest. Curry half-and-half for me. What about you?'

'Baffling me with science again, Bette. What would that be?'

'Curry, rice and chips.'

Sara felt her stomach turn. 'Okay, sounds fun.'

They had lunch in Newport and as prophesised, Sara did feel faintly ill watching Bette devour a beef curry with fat, greasy chips and a mass of white rice while she had chosen an unappetising dry salad that did nothing to assuage her appetite after the bracing air from the morning outside. She followed that with a couple of large chunks of bread and cheese that helped fill her stomach.

They arrived home mid-afternoon and battling against a strong wind, came in through the back door. Mike was in the downstairs lavatory and through the window saw them returning. He heard the door open as they entered. Carried by the wind behind her, he heard Bette say, 'My God, darling, who'd have babies when you can have freedom like this?'

He couldn't believe his ears. It wasn't only what she had said, but the way she had said it. She had delivered the line in such a disparaging tone and had laughed as she had said it. How *could* she profane Lucy's memory like that? How *could* she so disrespect their child in such an obscene, offensive way? And to say it to Sara like that.

In the evening they watched films on the television. Bette chose Graham Greene's *The End of the Affair*. Sara watched some of it then said she had to do some reading up on her Reiki course so, in spite of Bette's protests, managed to extricate herself from watching a film that was making her feel both sad and uncomfortable.

Mike avoided the women almost entirely, to the point where he had made an excuse that he had to go to Newport to get something and that he would grab supper there. He would not look at Bette and seemed deeply angry. Sara decided keeping out of his way was the wisest course of action whilst Bette seemed her usual oblivious self. She had such bad radar when it came to other people's feelings.

She felt something tight close over her mouth and stick hard to the skin of her cheeks which were drawn back, forcing her lips into an uncomfortable grimace. Unable to breathe either through her nose or mouth, her panic turned to terror that ran through her veins and petrified her.

Her thoughts grew muddled, her mind confused. What was

happening? Where was she? She seemed to be moving. Someone seemed to be leading her somewhere. To a car? Yes, to a car. To a car boot that was open. She was being pushed into it. She couldn't struggle because something was stopping her. She realised her hands were tied behind her back. She heard the boot door slam and felt the car move forward as her breathing and her heart slowed.

18

26 DECEMBER 2017. CLIFF EDGE

Incensed, that night Mike had no sleep. The remark of Bette's assaulted his mind over and over.

He began to wonder about a woman who speaks like that, especially when her baby had died. Suspicion stabbed his mind, filling it with poisonous thoughts. He tossed and turned, reliving that terrible time.

His thoughts searching for an escape route, he recalled every detail of what happened before and after the birth. He recalled the doctor at the maternity hospital mentioning that Bette had had a baby before. Surely a doctor couldn't make a mistake like that. Mike contemplated vile things.

But this was the woman he loved. Then he thought about that too. Because he had loved Bette, he had been living with the assumption that he must still love her, but was that the truth? Since Lucy had died, a thorny hedge had grown up between them and hidden the Bette he knew. Its roots had grown in their baby's dust. It was the line of defence they had both encouraged to shield themselves from the event and one another.

Only a new birth could bring that barrier down, thought Mike. But Bette had refused to try. *Why?* Why did she say she never wanted another baby? He began to wonder if she had ever really wanted Lucy in the first place.

He thought of her expression when she came out of the bathroom holding the pregnancy test. She hadn't actually looked happy. But he had been in such a hurry to find out, and when he had seen it was positive had been so over the moon, he had hardly noticed her reaction. But now he thought of it, what at the time he had considered to be delighted shock, could in fact have been undelighted shock.

As he lay in the dark, the wind hammering the house, he knew that when he really needed to, he could lie with the utmost sincerity. If he could, then why shouldn't Bette be able to, too?

His doubts about her grew larger and larger. Had anything she had told him about her past been true at all? He itched to know. A plan began to formulate.

19

27 DECEMBER 2017. PEMBROKESHIRE

Mike had been longing to go on one of his 'marathon' all-day walks. Today, tired though he was, adrenaline spiked his system and he rose early. He had told the others he intended to take the car to Poppit Sands then walk the coastal path to Newport Town and back to the Sands. He was determined, he said, to do the long round trip all in one day and in cold conditions. A twenty-two-miler with some very steep hills, even if they had wanted to be in his company, Bette and Sara would never consider joining him. He could be sure of that.

Relieved to get away from the women, after cooking himself a large breakfast, Mike took his knapsack with some food and maps and, reluctant even to speak to Bette, he muttered goodbye to her as she came downstairs in her dressing gown. The weather was still freezing but it was blue sky and yesterday's wind had dropped.

In his car by 8.28am, once Mike had reached the road, he turned right for St Dogmaels and drove slowly along, unconsciously whistling to himself. He always did this when he was tense and today, he was extremely apprehensive. But before he reached St Dogmaels, instead of heading left for Poppit Sands, he carried on until he came to Cardigan Bay. Circumnavigating the town, he looped back along the easternmost side of the bay where he finally reached a hotel high up on cliffs overlooking the sea.

By the time he drove to the car park, the weather had changed again. He felt something wet on his face and looked up at the heavy, white sky. As though it was holding back something in store and was simply teasing, it allowed a few slushy specks of snow to fall, melting the second they landed. The lackadaisical attempt stopped as quickly as it had started. But the weather was the last thing on his mind. Mike grabbed his knapsack from the passenger seat and strode into the hotel.

In the lounge that overlooked the bay, the lanky, methodical man removed his laptop from the knapsack, placed it carefully on the shiny, orange wooden table in front of him and opened it up. He straightened it in front of him. Organised as he loved to be, he had been sure to fully charge it before setting out and, in case the battery showed low, had brought the charger with him. Now he could peruse at his leisure. There was no one else in the place apart from an extremely gaunt, almost skeletal man who approached him and hovered nervously before taking courage and asking if he could get him anything.

'A double espresso, please,' said Mike.

The man looked aghast. 'I beg your pardon, sir?'

Repeating the sentence would be a waste of time, so Mike substituted with, 'Could I have a strong cup of black coffee, please.'

Looking relieved, the man said, 'Certainly sir.' He ambled out the room. There was no hurry to do anything in this hotel, in particular not at this time of year.

For a second, Mike wished Bette was with him to laugh at what would have been a quietly spoken, 'that's what you call a skeleton staff.' But she wasn't here, and he was here because of her. He felt hugely sad. The times when they had laughed so much together seemed so long ago.

He had ordered digitised copies of the *Western Telegraph*, the main local newspaper for Pembrokeshire. They were for the period from June through to September for the year of 2010 and 2011. He downloaded them on his laptop and searched for the words Bette and Davies with no luck. Then he entered 'couple' 'missing' and 'daughter.' He pored through countless mentions until, in a 2010 paper, he finally found something that set the hairs on the back of his neck tingling.

Beside a story in an issue from early September was a picture of Bette, younger but unmistakably her. Horrified by the headline, he slowly read the article.

Couple's Life Savings Stolen by daughter

Mr and Mrs Dai Davis of Llanegelly Farm, Hook, near Haverfordwest returned from a shopping trip on Thursday 29th August, to discover their sixteen-year-old daughter Bethan had disappeared from the family home.

When she made no appearance the following day, Mrs Davis had checked her daughter's bedroom to find some of her clothes and shoes gone. When she later checked she discovered to her horror that the couple's life savings of over £38,000 had disappeared.

Distrusting banks, the couple had hidden their money in a place known only to them so it had to have been Bethan.

Said Mrs Davis, 'We couldn't believe she'd just disappear like that. We don't know what came over the girl. But we still love her and even if she's spent the money, we'll get over that. We just want to know she's all right and get her home safe.'

Local taxi companies have no record of the girl booking a cab and it is assumed she must have taken a bus from somewhere near her home. But none of the local bus drivers have recognised her picture nor have any recollection of a girl with a suitcase boarding their bus.

The police search for Miss Davis continues. If anyone recognises this photograph and has seen Bethan in the last few days or has any information as to her whereabouts, please get in touch with the Police at Haverfordwest.

Astounded, Mike sat motionless in his chair and stared through the window at the bleak sea beyond. He tried to absorb what he had just read. The sky looked ready to burst with snow. The forecast on the car radio had said it was expected that afternoon. He reread the piece and gradually took in the information. They must have got her age wrong. She was now twenty-seven.

Anger surged through his body and he wanted to smash the computer that had relayed the knowledge. This had been much worse than he had been expecting. He felt duped, cheated, taken in. As he jotted down the name of the farm where the Davises lived, it crossed his mind that it might have been better if he hadn't found this out at all. To steal from her parents like that... What sort of person would do that?

He remembered what Bette had told him about how bad those parents were and he had tactfully avoided mentioning them ever since. Perhaps they had been worse than she had let on. Or perhaps it was the other way around. What was he to believe?

He bent his body forward, crossed his arms in front of him and laid his head on them. He slowly processed what he had read and the temper that had engulfed him calmed down. He had come up with a plan.

The skinny man came over to ask if he could get him anything else. Muttering that it had taken long enough to get one cup of coffee, and he didn't fancy waiting for another hour to get a second, Mike stood up. He slotted his computer into its weatherproof case, picked it up, left the hotel and walked back to his car. The weather felt colder than earlier.

Sitting in his car, he studied a map. He fed his next destination into his satnav which told him it would take about fifty-one minutes to drive there. Switching on his beloved Billie and now feeling more positive, he set off to follow the route back round Cardigan Bay, through the town and turned inland down a B road, along which he snatched longing glances at the tempting climbing country of the Preseli Hills off to his left.

As he drove, he went over the past. He thought of as much as he could remember of what Bette had told him about her childhood. Although he was beginning to doubt a single word was true he reminded himself to hang back from leaping to conclusions.

Descending as he drove across Pembrokeshire, Mike passed Haverfordwest where the fields had fewer sheep than in the north of the county: most land around that part was arable. He followed the banks of the river Cleddau on its way to Pembroke Dock as it widened and passed Hook. The satnav took him away from the village out into countryside along a narrow potholed lane that eventually led to the farm.

It was about 4.40pm and dark when he reached the end of the lane. He'd been expecting the large house described by Bette. But instead he found a small stone cottage. These were poor people. The place had the air of being deserted, but a yellow glow of light showed through the edges of closed curtains. For a moment he was reminded of the traveller in the spooky poem, *The Listeners*. Barking from more than one dog came from the house.

There was a long wait. He knocked again, louder and longer. More barking. Eventually, a short, grizzled, stocky man with a beer belly opened the door. Three collies stood close by, ready to spring.

'And who may you be?' This was said more warily than aggressively and he held a shotgun that, Mike was glad to note, was pointing to the ground. Above the grizzle, Bette's round blue eyes studied Mike.

Assuring the farmer that he meant no harm, Mike said politely, 'Good evening. Would you be Mr Davis, sir?'

The collies barked again. Mr Davis stroked their heads kindly and they quietened. 'Hush now, beauties. I am Dai Davis, that is me. More to the point, who are you and what will you be wanting?'

'My name is Michael Hanson and that's a long story, sir. May I ask you, whether your daughter went missing in August 2010?'

The man looked as though he'd seen a ghost. Lost for words, he tottered on his feet for a moment. Thinking he might fall, Mike caught hold of his arm. 'I'm sorry if I've shocked you, sir.'

'No one's mentioned Bethan for years now. Why would you be asking?'

His eyes were watering. Mike asked whether he might come in and have a talk. The shaken man leant his rabbit gun against the wall by the door and invited him in. He gestured Mike to sit in an ancient high-backed chair beside an old pot-bellied stove.

Then Mr Davis pointed at the floor. 'Down,' he said and the dogs immediately dropped at his feet, not taking their eyes off their owner. He patted their heads and ruffled the hair on their chests. Not quite the cruel man Bette had described.

Offered tea, Mike accepted with gratitude. While Mr Davis put an old-fashioned kettle on a ring of an electric cooker, Mike took in the room. Built of mostly old grey stones of various shapes and sizes, the fireplace had a thick, slightly misshapen old beam roughly hewn into an arch that stretched between two pillars. The thickness of the walls was visible in the window recess about twenty inches deep. Built to keep out the cold, this was a cosy room that might have been unchanged for a hundred years apart from the electric cooker.

He could imagine a restless, creative child being bored in this out-of-the-way spot. He remembered Bette's tale of painting her bedroom. Not in this house: she couldn't have as it was all bare stone walls. Not a hint of magnolia anywhere. He wondered whether he was living with a fantasist.

He thought to ask, 'Er, excuse me, sir, but is there a Mrs Davis?'

'Died these seven years since.' As he brought a tray with two cups, a bowl of sugar and a teapot, Dai Davis looked beaten, like a man who has given up.

'I am so very sorry to hear that, sir.'

The man had more tears in his eyes. He fished a dirty handkerchief from his pocket and wiped them. Before he sat down, he poured them both a cup of tea. It crossed Mike's mind that the man may have loved his wife but not his daughter.

'All of them, see? All my girls gone. Now I've no one. Although they said it was the cancer, I'm sure as eggs is eggs, my poor wife died of a broken heart.'

They sat in silence drinking tea while Mike wondered what he had meant by 'all his girls'. He was trying to decide how to approach what was clearly going to be a much trickier subject than he had been expecting when Mr Davis paved the way for him. 'So what do you know of our Bethan, then?'

'Er, Mr Davis, I'm afraid you are going to need to be patient while I explain how I know her.'

'You *know* her? You mean, she's *alive*? Are you *sure*? There'll be a many Bethan Davises in Wales, you know. I reckon you've made a mistake, young man.' The poor man was aghast.

'The Bethan Davis who took your life savings?'

It seemed he couldn't absorb what Mike was saying. 'Well,

she was only young, mind, and if she had lived, she'd have repaid us. She was a good girl our Bethan and I'll never believe she ran off without good cause. Doctor said she may have been what they call depressed, you know. We're certain she took her own life, you see. You're barking up the wrong tree, son.'

He called Mike 'young man' and 'son', but Mike decided that in spite of his weather-beaten, grizzled appearance, that he couldn't be more than fifty.

Mike made a decision then and there that he couldn't tell this sad, lonely man the truth. 'I believe you're right, sir. I think I must be mistaken. I am so sorry to have disturbed and upset you. Please forgive me.'

'Well, well, I was truly shaken then, when you said what you did.'

'I can believe it. As I'm here, tell me about your daughter, anyway. I'm so sorry to hear she had such an unhappy end. Did you have other children?'

Mike prayed the man would forget to wonder how he had known about the life savings being missing. And he did. He was a simple-living man whose life had been devastated. All he was now thinking about were his late wife and daughter.

'No, never did. Mother kept miscarrying see and Bethan was the only one to stay put. A lovely little girl she was.' He got up and crossed the room to bring a gold plastic frame enclosing a photograph over to show Mike. 'Pretty as a picture, wasn't she?'

A ten-year-old Bette smiled a toothier smile than she had grown into – but she and the smile were as dazzling then as now.

'She was indeed.' Not wishing to seem too eager to find out more, Mike paused. 'And she obviously had a loving home so I can't help wondering why she left and what happened.'

'Clever child. Very artistic, you know. We couldn't buy enough paper, paints and crayons for her. She just loved drawing and painting and we encouraged her all we could. Even scraped together to pay the local artist to give her lessons. And then...' His eyes narrowed. 'Local lad to blame. Got her pregnant then ran out on her. She was only fifteen, poor kid. Well, she had the babe at home and we cared for them both. But poor young Bethan, she found it very hard to cope, see? That's what drove her away. The babi was barely three months at the time. The doctor told us childbirth can affect the mind, you see.'

'So when she disappeared, how old was she?'

'Only just had her sixteenth birthday.' He was sniffing back tears again. 'My poor lamb.'

Some quick mental arithmetic told Mike that the paper had been correct and that Bette was now only twenty-three years old. She'd said she was twenty-five when they had met in 2014. He couldn't believe it. She had actually been twenty. She'd looked young but always seemed so grown up. From spending years fending for herself, he presumed. *Such a convincing liar. She'd never had a passport and had refused to apply for one as she would have had to produce documents to prove her birth. She claimed this was because she did not want her parents to find out where she was.*

'It must have been terrible for you and your wife.'

'It was. But Mother and I kept Beth's little Rhiannon and we loved her like our own. Course, once Mother got so ill, we had to put the baby up for adoption. But we keep in touch and she knows her true story, so that's something, and she sometimes comes visiting. She's all I have left of the family now, so I treasure the time I spend with her.'

'What can I say, sir? I am so sorry about everything you've had to bear.' Mike stood up.

'Sorry you've had a wasted journey, young man. Good luck with your search.'

Pausing on the doorstep, Mike wanted to hug the man and tell him his darling daughter was fine. But he mustn't. Why overturn what the man believed for the truth? It would only make him unhappy. It was surely better for him to believe his daughter had died in tragic circumstances and that none of it had been her fault.

'Thank you very much, Mr Davis. Good luck to you too and goodnight.'

When Mike went out into the darkness, it was full-on snowing and this time it was settling. This was snow in earnest. He glanced at his watch. Would the women be wondering what had happened to him? He thought he should call but couldn't face speaking to that lying bitch. To think he had once loved her. But not anymore, not anymore. Local lad got her into trouble? Local lad she had seduced, more like. He knew just how flirtatious and now just how deceitful she could be. He sent her the shortest text he could. Just four brief words, no kisses.

On my way back.

By the time he was back on the larger road, the snow was coming fast and thick. Grateful for the four-wheel drive in his car, he wondered whether he'd ever make it back to Cliff Edge as other traffic was likely to get into trouble en route.

He thought about how sometimes it was definitely preferable for people to believe what they wanted, but at other times vital that they learnt the truth. He suddenly realised that he was no different from poor Mr Davis. He had believed what he wanted to.

As he drove, his windscreen wipers at full speed, he began to think about Lucy's death. Who had been the last to check on her that night? The whole thing had been such a shock that self-protection had leapt to his aid and blocked such details from his memory. He just had to get back.

Bette had left one baby and the second had died at about the same age.

The fury in him boiled. He wanted to hit out and his fists clenched the steering wheel so hard it might almost have snapped. Finally, with a scream of his brakes, he jerked the wheel over, pulling the car to the side of the road, stopped, got out and slammed the door. Slanting snowfall covered every bit of him as he stood in darkness and let out an animal roar. Cold flakes entered his mouth and melted on contact.

Gradually, he talked himself down. He must hold this raging stress inside until it could be allowed full vent. That time was coming soon. Mike Hanson had had just about all he could take.

Disorientated though she was, she was aware of the car stopping. Where were they? It was hard to see and she was so, so cold. For what purpose had they stopped? Instinct, still working at some level, knew the purpose was bad. Fear flooded through her veins and froze her blood. Her heart and breathing had already slowed and her mouth felt as though it was filled with sand. Desperately thirsty, she craved water.

When the boot opened, the bitter cold bit her face and hands and her sluggish mind and body were unable to resist the hands that pulled her out and the voice that ordered her to stand. More tape was stuck around her face and over her nose. Now she couldn't breathe at all. Panic overwhelmed her.

She tried to struggle but staggered and stumbled as she was pulled along into deep snow where her knees buckled and she fell into a deep white drift. There she lay, as consciousness slipped away.

Snow and darkness covered her. She did not feel the tape ripped away from her face for Death was already on her.

20

7 JANUARY 2018, 2.55PM. CLIFF EDGE

The three police officers leave Fishguard with Evans at the wheel in his car, Jane beside him and PC Rhys Roberts in the rear.

They take the road to the right towards Dinas Cross. It is a remote lane, narrow and twisted with tall hedgerows either side. Evans spends a lot of time on the horn until Jane shushes him. 'You can't keep doing that, Evans, people will notice us. We're not in Carmarthen now. This is the countryside. We need to catch the woman by surprise.'

Evans is clearly worried about the possibility of another car coming toward them and slows to a crawl. Another of his failings: he can be a real wuss. They zigzag along the rutted lane as it follows the coastline. Before long, Jane reminds Evans, 'It's just here, see. On the left, remember? That's the track that leads to the place.'

They drive up the bumpy track towards Cliff Edge. There are no cars outside. They try the door but no one's home.

'We'll wait somewhere out of sight and keep watch on the place. Turn us around please, Evans. We need to catch Ms de Vries by surprise.'

He does as bid, driving back up the track onto the lane where they go down a quarter mile until Jane points out a well-hidden gap into which Evans reverses the car. They get out and stroll back along the lane.

'Suppose to all intents and purposes we look like people on a country walk,' says Evans.

'Except for the uniformed officer with us.' Sometimes Jane wonders how Evans got into the police let alone gained the position he is now in. But she knows he's actually got a good brain when he remembers to engage it.

They climb over a stone wall and head for a small group of trees, a little way from the house. They hide in the cover of the trees, binoculars trained on the place. It's perishing cold but they don't have too long to wait. At 15:49 a silver Ford Fiesta that has seen better days rattles down the track. It stops at Cliff Edge and a blonde woman gets out.

'That's who I spoke to,' says Roberts, his teeth chattering.

'Yes, that's her, isn't it, Evans?'

'It is, ma'am.'

They watch the woman open the boot and take out some carrier bags with what looks like groceries. She goes to the front door and lets herself in. The police wait until after a couple of minutes, they walk to their car and drive back up the track again to park next to the house.

Jane and Evans get out of the car and go to the door. Jane checks her watch as she knocks. They'll be driving back in the dark, not much fun on the icy roads, especially with Evans, jumpy as a cat, at the wheel. The door opens. As it does, Jane gets a call from PC Thomas in Fishguard but she clicks her phone off. Not a good moment to talk.

She holds up her badge. 'Ms de Vries? You will remember us from when we met just three days ago. I was asking about Gwyneth Edwards who has, unfortunately, not yet been found.

But we are here on a different matter this time. I am Detective Inspector Jane Owen. This is Detective Sergeant Ross Evans' – she gestures at Evans who nods his head – 'and you will remember Constable Roberts who visited you earlier today.'

'Yes,' replies the woman.

'Good afternoon. May we come in, please? We just want to talk to you and ask you some questions, if that's all right?'

Reserved, polite but clearly nervous, she says, 'Yes, of course. Come in.'

Two dogs run to the door as Jane, Evans and Roberts step through the porch and then through another door into the expansive, open-plan, kitchen-living room. Jane glances about for photographs of the couple who own the house but there are none visible. Sara motions the dogs to their beds and they comply at once.

'Shall we sit at the table?' She motions Sara to take the seat next to her, while the two men sit across from the woman. 'Sara.' Jane smiles warmly at her. 'This property, known as Cliff Edge, is listed as owned by...' – she consults her notes – 'a Mr Michael Hanson. I understand from what you told us before that you are friends of his and his partner, a Ms Bette Davies. Is that correct?'

'Well, not exactly. I'm a friend of Bette's, not so much Mike's.'

'But you are currently staying with them here. Are the owners back now?'

'Er, no.'

'Having checked my notes from when I saw you regarding the disappearance of Gwyneth Edwards, you told me they were hiking in Snowdonia for two nights. So where are they now?'

'They never came back. Just disappeared.'

Jane raises her eyebrows. 'Disappeared?' She has warned the others that she will make no mention of the drowned body at this stage. '*Both* of them?'

'I told your officer earlier. I'm very afraid so. I can explain what little I know.'

'I am sorry to hear that and, that being the case, I must ask you to accompany us to our temporary police headquarters in Fishguard for the purposes of an interview. Would you be agreeable to that?'

The surprised woman asks, 'But am I in trouble for some reason? I had nothing to do with anything, I can assure you.'

'You're in no trouble at all, Sara. None at all. It is just that in the case that we are investigating, the possible disappearance of two people, we would need to do a formal interview. You can always refuse if you so wish, but you would need to be aware that that could affect our perception of you as a witness.'

'Of course. I understand completely. I'm happy to come to the station. When were you thinking?'

'Well, I'm afraid it has to be now, Sara. I'm sorry, but in the case of a disappearance, or in this case two disappearances, time is of the essence. You are, of course, at liberty to refuse but it might look as though you were trying to hide something if you did.'

'Right, of course, I understand.'

'We can drive you there right away and run you back here later, if you are agreeable.'

A flicker of something crosses Sara's face. Irritation or something else? Jane is unsure. Irritation would be unsurprising, if that was what it was.

Jane insists on travelling in the back next to Sara. They chat on the way to Fishguard. Evans' nervousness at the wheel is worse than ever in the dark, but Jane firmly disregards it. She senses a relatively relaxed aura about her witness. Not the behaviour of a guilty person.

They reach the town hall by 5.30pm and guide Sara into the 'interview room', an area cordoned off with screens. It has a trestle table set up with six chairs around it.

Jane sits down, nods at Roberts to sit Sara opposite her. He then leaves while Evans is fiddling about with an extension lead, plugging in the portable interview recorder. It has a battery but Evans, so lacking in care with his appearance but so careful in his job, prefers to plug in his equipment in case of battery failure. Jane smiles. 'May we offer you a cup of tea or coffee? We have some biscuits too, if you are hungry?'

Jane nods at Evans who crosses to the kitchen area and switches on the electric kettle. She needs to put Sara at ease. The more relaxed she is, the more she is likely to slip up if she is not telling the truth. She always makes sure to show her interviewees respect and talk to them as a friend: that way they are more likely to be forthcoming.

'I just hope this won't take too long as I worry about my dog. She's a rescue and very nervous if she's not with me.'

'We shouldn't be too long. Don't worry, Sara. I'm sure the dog will be okay. She's with the other one, isn't she?'

'Yes, but...'

Evans has finally sorted the machine to his satisfaction. He shuffles round to take the chair on Jane's left and places the recorder in front of him. He is fidgety. Jane taps his knee under the table. He glances at her and she says with a hint in her tone, 'All settled now, Detective Evans?'

Over time, he has learnt to absorb his boss's innuendos. He stills himself.

Jane says, 'This recording, Sara, is just for our records. As you can imagine, we have to be so careful to recall witness statements, and this is the only accurate way of doing it.'

She continues. 'Ms de Vries. First of all, before we get to the matter in hand, we need to know a little more about you. Do you understand? Would you mind telling us where you live and what you do for a living?'

'I live in Cambridge, which is where I got to know Bette, and I am a massage therapist.'

'How interesting,' says Jane. 'So what do you do exactly?'

'I offer deep tissue massage, Indian head massage, pregnancy massage, sports massage, holistic massage, hot stone massage and acupressure massage. I tailor each treatment session to each client and can combine techniques from different aspects of these therapies to create a bespoke treatment.'

'Impressive. And can you give us your national insurance number if you know it, your date of birth, address and telephone number.'

'You can write them down here.' Evans passes Sara a witness statement form. She fills in the details.

'And how did you meet Bette Davies?'

'Dog walking. We just hit it off at once and became very good friends.'

'Right. So, I understand that you stayed at Cliff Edge over Christmas and have been there since then.'

Evans pipes up. 'The witness is nodding her head.'

'So where do you believe Mr Hanson and Ms Davies to be currently?'

'I have no idea where either of them are.'

'Why do you say that, Sara?'

'Because they both went off and never returned. I have tried calling and calling their mobiles with no luck. I'm frightened that one or both of them are dead.'

Sara wells up with tears that start slowly then run down her cheeks.

There would normally be a cube of tissues at the ready in the police station but no such luxuries in the town hall. 'Evans, could you find some tissues for Ms de Vries, please.'

He walks over to the kitchen area and returns with a roll of paper towels. 'Sorry, love.' He shrugs but looks sympathetic. 'Best I can do.'

Sara takes the roll, tears off a sheet and wipes her eyes. 'I think something awful happened. I think he may have hurt her, even have done away with her.'

Jane's mind fills with the smell of burning and she sees her father's blackened body in the hospital mortuary. She blinks hard and her head feels swimmy. She puts her head in her hands. The vision clears and she is back in the room. She looks up and realises they are waiting for her to speak.

'So what makes you say that?'

Sara gives her a strange look before continuing. 'Well, there was a very bad atmosphere between the couple throughout the Christmas period and then late in the evening of December 27th, they had a really bad row.'

'Can you tell me what the argument was about?'

'Well, I can't say exactly as I was in my room but I heard the word, 'money' and stuff about their child. They thought I was asleep at the time. They had been devastated by the loss of their baby in the spring of last year and both had been deeply unhappy ever since. It was a cot death. A terrible thing. I would say it took very little to set them off. They were definitely having relationship problems. Bette confided in me. She told me Mike had a hell of a temper and he made it fairly obvious he wanted to spend as little time as possible with her or me. I know poor Bette tried hard to get their relationship back on track but he didn't seem to want to cooperate.'

Jane feels a sharp pang of sympathy for anyone losing their baby in such a ghastly way. She pushes away the emotion.

Detecting a faint trace of foreign accent, she guesses this woman may be Scandinavian. She jots away on a notepad while Evans keeps his eyes on Sara's face as she sobs. Now she has started on her account, she doesn't seem to be able to stop.

'The next thing I know is Mike running downstairs...'

'How do you know it was Mr Hanson and not Ms Davies?'

'Mike and not Bette? Well, it was heavy-footed you know and I heard Bette call something after him. I got worried at this stage as there was quite a blizzard that evening and if Mike planned to drive, it could have been very dangerous.

That was when I threw on my dressing gown and ran downstairs to try to stop him. But he had already left the house and was moving towards his car. I grabbed my coat and hastily put on my boots and ran out in the snow to follow him. He heard my shouts and stopped.

Then we both got into his car where I managed to persuade him to calm down and not to drive that night. He finally agreed it was a mad idea, but he was so angry, you see. Anyway, thank goodness, he came back into the house with me and I persuaded him to talk it through with Bette in the morning.

He knew it was the wise thing to do, so he stayed the night on the big couch. I went to bed relieved that I'd been able to stop him driving in a state in such shocking weather conditions.'

'And can you tell us what happened then?'

'Well, as you may imagine I was embarrassed to be there with them at this point and kept out of the way, but we all muddled through, Mike sleeping on the couch until the 31st when I came down in the morning to find a note in Mike's handwriting. It said that they were going away for a couple of nights to Snowdonia to hike and talk things over. There was a fair amount of snow on the lanes and a high wind was blowing it into drifts. It didn't seem the right conditions to be going up there at all, but they'd left, so what could I do? They left me the keys and plenty of food. And they'd left their dog. By the evening of the third day–'

'This was January 2nd?' interrupts Jane to clarify.

'Yes,' the blonde woman agrees. By the evening of January 2nd they didn't return and by the following morning I was beginning to fret. Then I got a call from Mike on the 3rd saying they were fine and hoped I wouldn't mind if they stayed a bit longer and that they would let me know when they'd be back.'

She now sobs uncontrollably. Jane nods to Evans who hands the distressed woman another piece of kitchen roll.

'But, Sara, did you think of calling us?'

'I didn't know what to do. I mean it was only four days ago Mike called and said, "a bit longer." Well, what's "a bit longer"? But now their phones are both dead. I was going to call you. I would have done so today but you lot beat me to it.'

'Don't suppose by any chance you still have the note Mr Hanson left for you?'

'As a matter of fact I do, at Cliff Edge.'

'Lucky for us. We'll collect it later. Also, do you happen to know the couple's Cambridge address?'

'It may seem very odd, but I have never been to their house. I am a friend of Bette's... We walked the dogs together, occasionally had lunch at a farm café but didn't visit one another's homes. I know it was north of the river and near Midsummer Common, as Bette told me. I think it was a road beginning with a K – Kin or King something, but I don't know the actual address.' Slow tears ease down her pale cheeks. 'Please tell me I'm not under suspicion, am I?' She looks apprehensive.

'You must understand, Sara, that your story is all we have to go on at the moment and that the police only work with facts. Once we have followed up and hopefully traced Mr Hanson and Ms Davies alive or otherwise, we will be better placed to answer that question.'

Jane decides there is no point in keeping the truth from her now. She nods at Evans who passes her a folder from which she removes photographs and spreads them on the tabletop. Jane will tell her now and watch her reaction.

'We can't be certain who it is just yet but we have retrieved a woman's body from the Witches' Cauldron.'

Watching the woman closely she says, 'Do you recognise any of these items, Sara?'

Sara wipes her tearful eyes and looks at the photos. She seems to think about the pictures before answering. This may mean she has been taken by surprise. Delays in answering can imply that people are dreaming up answers that may be far from the truth. It could, on the other hand, mean the woman is being careful in case she misidentifies the things. She scans the pictures with care. Then, suddenly she gulps for breath and her hands involuntarily fly to her face. 'Oh my God!' She points to a picture. 'This looks like Bette's coat.' She starts to tremble. Her eyes dart back to another of the photographs. 'And she definitely has a necklace like that with a cross on but it's silver. Oh God, did these come from the body you recovered?'

'They did.' Jane quickly places another three photos on the table. 'These are grim, I'm afraid, but I have to ask, do you recognise any of these?'

The photos show one of the distended corpse and two close-ups of the remains of the face.

Sara reels with shock. She looks as though she may throw up. For a while she seems unable to speak. She rocks gently in her chair before stopping to sit in silence and stare across the room, an expression of misery on her face. Jane reaches out in sympathy and touches her arm again. 'Would you like some water, Sara?'

The shaken woman stammers her reply and Evans nips to

the kitchenette to find a paper cup of water which he quickly hands to her.

Jane has done with the sympathy card for the moment. She does not intend to let up. 'Can you look at the pictures again, please.'

Sara forces herself to look again.

'Are you able to identify the person in any of these photographs?'

'I think it's Bette, but I just can't say for certain. I mean without the eyes...' – she shudders and looks away – 'if it is her, although she's virtually unrecognisable, but I suppose on balance from the shape of the face and the hair I would say it probably is.' Now she doubles up in grief and more tears spill out of her already red eyes.

Jane says, 'Do you by any chance have any photo of her on your phone?'

'Erm...' Between sobs and hesitating, she manages to say, 'I have some of her and of both of them taken at Christmas.' Still trembling slightly as she searches through her phone photos and finds them.

Jane cannot help glancing at her watch under the table. She is worrying about Meg and needs to get home. 'May I ask you to send me a copy of that picture, please.' Jane hands over her personal mobile number. 'This number may prove useful to you anyway, as you may remember things you have forgotten to say today or need to contact me for any other reason. And also before we return to Cliff Edge, we will need to take your DNA and fingerprints just for our records and to rule you out of any involvement.'

'Of course, I completely understand.'

Watching her closely, Jane notices that Sara doesn't blink and seems perfectly happy to allow a PC to swab the inside of her mouth and then to take her fingerprints.

'And we will have to ask for your mobile which we'll get back to you tomorrow, soon as we've checked it over.'

Now the woman baulks. 'But I can't stay at that house all alone without a mobile. I mean, what if Mike tries to call me? There's no landline there and I just wouldn't feel safe.'

'I am going to ask a couple of officers to stay overnight outside the house, so if there's any emergency, you can ask them to call.'

Sara looks down at her furry boots. Her head hangs and she starts to cry again. She is shaking. 'This all makes me feel as though you think I'm guilty of something. That you even think I might have had something to do with Bette's death. I loved her. And I can tell you that I absolutely did not. If only I'd called you right away when they didn't return, I think you wouldn't be so suspicious of me.'

'I'm afraid life is full of if onlys, Sara.'

They sit quietly in the car as Evans drives them back to Cliff Edge. Sara is numb with shock.

When they get back, the dogs greet Sara with great excitement. The officers wait while she lets them out and feeds them a late supper. Sara then goes straight to the kitchen where she opens a drawer and takes out a note.

How very helpful she is, thinks Jane who watches her crossing the room. She seems relaxed, perhaps it's the police presence. She hands the folded note to Jane who reads it.

We've decided to take a couple of nights hiking in Snowdonia. We'll stay at pubs or B&Bs. We think we need some time together to talk things through. So sorry for everything. We'll sort it out. Here's the keys and some money for food and extras. Mrs Edwards's son is dropping her off on the 2nd at 2.30. She'll do three hours and if we're not back, can you please let her in and pay her £12 per hour then run her home to Moylegrove afterwards? Sorry to ask and to leave you alone. Hope you'll be ok. Call if any problems.

Take care and see you soon, Mike & Bette x

This could be anyone's writing, thinks Jane. 'Out of interest,' she asks, 'I was just wondering what your reason was for keeping the note? After all, it was just a casual few sentences, not of any great importance, I imagine.'

'I was about to chuck it, but their disappearance was so peculiar I suppose you could say it was a kind of insurance in case no one believed me. Also, I wanted to keep a record of what I'd paid Mrs Edwards just so they knew I'd done so as asked.'

'Do you by any chance have anything else written by Mr Hanson, where we can compare the handwriting?'

Sara thinks for a while then suddenly seems uncomfortable and wriggles in her seat. She looks down at her clenched hands on the table in front of her. They tighten a bit more. She repeats the question while she thinks and then says, 'Well, I myself don't personally but Bette did once show me a billet-doux from him to her that she always kept in her wallet. She said if ever she doubted that he loved her, she would fish it out and read it.'

She crosses the room again, this time to the porch where an expensive brown leather shoulder bag is hanging on a coat hook. She unhooks it and brings it over to the table.

'I feel bad about handing it to you. It has Bette's private things in it.' She hands it to Evans who opens it and removes a crocodile-skin wallet. He fumbles through receipts and notes to find an old, well-worn, single page letter. It is written in an unusually precise hand, the letters beautifully formed and evenly spaced. He places it on the table between Jane and himself.

My darling, You are the light and the love of my life and always will be.

Yours for ever, Mike.

It certainly looks to be the same handwriting as on the note. Although only an expert could tell if the same person wrote both the note and the love letter.

Jane turns to Rhys. 'Come with me please, Roberts.' The constable follows her upstairs while Evans remains with Sara. They go into what is obviously the main bedroom. On a dressing table there are a man's and a woman's hairbrushes along with a silver framed photo of the couple with their arms around one another. She points to them and Roberts dons some latex gloves. He picks up the brushes and photo frame and drops them carefully in plastic bags. Also with gloves on, Jane closely examines the bed pillows. Finding a couple of strands of blonde hair as well as a short brown one, she pops them into separate bags as well.

On one of the bedside tables, there is a thick, padlocked, five-year diary. In the drawer of the table she finds a small key that fits the lock. Jane opens the diary and is unsurprised to see it is Bette's. She slips that into a bag, too. Then they go into the bathroom where there are a couple of toothbrushes. Roberts slips them into two more bags.

There is little left to ask the woman downstairs. She is being a helpful witness and Jane's gut tells her to believe her. Whether her story is true or not, they need to find Mike Hanson and they need to take all the trekking poles in Cliff Edge to Max Granger, the pathologist, to see what he can make of them. She doesn't explain her reasons for putting plastic bags round the bottoms of them. Sara looks surprised when they do this, but not unduly bothered.

Jane shakes her hand and asks her to remain in Cliff Edge while they continue to conduct their enquiries.

The woman looks relieved to have got her story off her chest, if not to be asked to remain in this lonely place. Her brow puckers. 'Am I safe to stay here alone?'

To reassure her, Jane curls a gentle hand around Sara's forearm. 'We'll be watching the place in case Mr Hanson decides to return. Which, I am certain he won't. He knows we will be looking for him sooner or later and this is the last place he is likely to come back to. Don't worry, Sara, you'll be safe here. You have the officers outside and you can ask them to call me any time night or day. You'll have your phone back tomorrow. And it won't be long before you'll be able to return to Cambridge.'

'Oh thank you, thank you.' She is crying again.

21

7 JANUARY 2018. CARMARTHEN

Meg Owen is used to pain. She had been taught methods of coping with it by the pain clinic in the rehab unit.

Nowadays, the original agony has left her except for occasional sharp twinges down her right arm, but here it is again. *Hello pain,* she sings in her head, *my old friend.* But what she will never get used to is hospitals. Their sounds, their atmosphere but most of all their smells.

She gazes at the hurting wrist lying on her lap and tries the meditation trick. But there is too much noise in the A&E department for her to concentrate. One woman is moaning in agony from something wrong with her stomach; and a small child screams and cries as the result of a bleeding wound in his arm which has a large piece of glass sticking out of it.

Carys won't stop chattering as usual and Meg wishes she was anywhere other than where she is. But if there is one thing she has mastered it is both mental and physical tolerance. Once, when a visiting friend had remarked on her bravery and how in spite of everything she carried on, she had snapped, 'I don't exactly have a choice, do I?' and had regretted it afterwards. She had since made a personal vow to herself never to put her problems on others as mostly all they wanted to do was help. But the vow didn't always work.

At times, she *does* feel sorry for herself, very sorry for herself, and at others she yearns for – aches for – her mam, and occasionally she feels like giving up the fight. But by and large, though, she manages well to be cheerful, knowing it is her best chance of having a half-reasonable life.

Another thing Meg has recently recognised is that she cannot go on for ever relying on Jane. It isn't fair on her hard-working sister. Perhaps if she can become more independent, she might find a life she can properly enjoy. She feels ready now. She dreams of driving to a job and being a normal person, like everyone else. She is tired of being pitied and called 'dear' and patronised as though she is very old and hard of hearing. Because that's what happens when a person's in a wheelchair.

The first thing she needs to do is to find a disabled driving instructor to give her lessons in an adapted car. Then she needs to pass the test, then to apply for a car. Yes, she must now start to fight for an independent life of her own. She might even meet a man. Or better still, reunite with the boyfriend she had before the accident ruined everything. They had been deeply in love at the time. She still often fantasises and dreams about him and is always deeply despondent when she has to wake up to reality. Now, the memory of him thrills her and her mind is enjoying an afternoon of passion with him in the garden shed while her mother is out.

'Meg Owen?' She is jolted back to reality and automatically takes hold of the wheels of her chair. A vicious pain shoots through her wrist, causing her to let out a cry.

'Now Meg, let me do that, let me do that.' Carys grabs the wheelchair handles and they follow a disgruntled nurse to a cubicle. The nurse is not actually disgruntled, she just looks it because she is exhausted. Nearing the end of what has turned out to be an extra-long shift, she longs to get home, stuff her face with a large meal and fall straight to sleep afterwards.

When the doctor arrives some twenty minutes later, Meg is sent to X-ray. Carys, still nattering, follows the nurse as she wheels Meg.

Diagnosed with a scaphoid fracture, Meg has her wrist encased in a plaster of Paris cast and is told it can be removed in six to twelve weeks. Once they have seen her, she is given a prescription for some painkillers and discharged with an appointment for six weeks' time and a letter for her doctor.

The plaster cast is "a darned nuisance", as Meg's mother used to say. The other hand, although better and working relatively well, is still affected by the shoulder injury and she has had to learn to brush her hair with her left hand. *Ah well,* she tells herself, *Jane can do it in the mornings.*

She thinks about her sister with deep affection. Although she didn't always remember to appreciate Jane, Meg knows just how wonderful she is to her. She feels a pang of concern for her since she is very distracted. Apparently, she is leading an ongoing murder investigation and it's the first time as boss when such a thing has happened on her 'patch'.

Meg knows talking will help relieve some of the stress she can tell Jane is under and she is determined to get her sister, who is not really supposed to discuss cases outside the force, to tell more. Talk and Scrabble are their main things in the evenings and the discussions they share are more vital to Meg than she knows. They talk about all sorts from matters of the heart to the state of the world. Like Radio Four, they help her remain in touch with the outside world. So it cuts both ways, helping Jane deal with pressure and Meg to maintain interest in life.

~

When they leave Cliff Edge, Jane calls Fishguard and asks for PC Thomas. He tells her that on his search of the arched part of the rock that straddles the watery sea cave he has found a discarded mobile phone in the grass.

'Well done, Thomas. Very well done. So that needs to be got over to Llangunnor as soon as possible. Get the SIM in the kiosk to extract the data. Hopefully, it may be related to this case but if not, it could be something else fishy. The sooner we get to see the contents, the better. Thanks again, Thomas. I hope you've ensured the phone has not been mishandled in any way. By the way, what sort of phone is it and what colour?'

'It's a gold iPhone. I've been very careful, indeed I have, ma'am. Only thing is it's been under snow for a time, so I don't know...' She is too tired to listen to Thomas ramble.

'Good man, bye for now.'

From the car, she calls Sara. 'Sorry to trouble you again so soon, Sara, but I wondered whether you could tell me what Bette's phone looked like?'

'Yes, I can. It was an iPhone.'

'And would you recall the colour?'

'Gold,' says Sara.

Take her by surprise, thinks Jane. 'And there's just one more question I meant to ask before. Why stay in Cliff Edge once they'd gone? Why not return to your own home earlier?'

'I wanted to take Bette's dog with me back to my flat, but I'd already gone through hoops with pleading to be allowed one well-behaved dog and the landlord would never allow me to have two – that's rented property in Cambridge for you. Also, I could never get away with two dogs at my job. I had decided to wait a little while longer in hope that one or both would get in touch. But, as I told you, I have heard nothing. I don't know what to do about Brynn. He's such a lovely dog and I'd like to keep him. The two dogs have become inseparable. And this place is so perfect for them. But of course, I have to get back to Cambridge soon. It's a real quandary. But now' – there is a choke in her voice – 'with poor Bette being dead, I shall have to keep him. I'll just have to find somewhere outside Cambridge that will allow two dogs.'

Jane thanks her for her help, asks her to stay a few days longer and assures her the police guard will remain at Cliff Edge.

On the way back to Llangunnor to go to their various homes, Jane is quiet in the car. She thinks through the interview. She knows better than to trust every word a witness says. While there's no simple way to discern the difference between a stressed-out, innocent person from a criminal trying to trick you, Jane is inclined to believe Sara is telling the truth. But she never bases a case solely on what a witness says. They could, after all, be a suspect. She encouraged Sara to tell her story in narrative form so that later when asked to repeat it, if it was not the truth, she might make a mess of the details.

Jane imagines that Bette's killer is either desperate, jealous or angry. For all she knows, this Sara may have bumped off the couple and have been planning to take over their house in Wales with no one knowing. But once the police showed up, she may have had to alter her plans. Jane must treat her as though she is a clever, cunning murderer. But then again, if she was a murderer, why would she alert the police? If it was her that rang them? But who else was it? Perhaps some passer-by? They had dusted the phone box, found some fingerprints with no match. That would have been the last thing she would have done.

Jealousy stood out as the obvious motive but since the woman was seriously upset or the equivalent of an Oscar-winning actress, Jane decides for the moment to believe Sara... for now.

Her thoughts turn to the mobile phone. Who would leave a

phone up at the Witch's Cauldron unless it was to deliberately lose the thing? Maybe someone meant to throw it in the sea but the wind blew it back and prevented it from going down? So much to think about. She is looking forward to reading Bette's diary. Maybe there'll be a clue or two in there. This is far from a clear-cut case.

The trouble is she's fussing about Meg. This keeps interrupting her usually clear patterns of thought. What a time for such a thing to happen. When she's investigating a case of murder. She tells herself the cold light of day will help and so will seeing Meg.

She has again had a flashback while interviewing the de Vries woman. It won't do. She can't let it start happening again, but how can it be stopped? She will call the counsellor when she has a free moment.

Evans hums and plays his fingers on the steering wheel, both of which irritate but she manages to avoid saying anything. She knows he only does it to relax himself. She blanks him out as she needs to go deep into the act of remembering just about everything Sara said. Of course, she will be able to listen back to the recording the following day but for now, she wants to think over the interview. It's not just *what* a person says; it's *how* they say it. She's good at both verbal and physical recall which helps a great deal if you're in the police. Did Sara say or do anything to incriminate herself? *No, she didn't.* Had her body language given anything away? *No, it hadn't.*

The main thing that has disturbed Jane was the fact that the woman had not reported the couple's disappearance. Any decent citizen would surely have got the info to the police earlier.

By the time Jane gets home it is 8.10pm. She rushes from her car to the bungalow front door, almost slipping on the ice as she does. *Slow down,* she tells herself. *Another couple of seconds won't make any difference at all.* She collects herself and as she approaches the bungalow starts fretting as there are no lights on.

She runs in to see a note left on the kitchen table.

Doc said I'd better go to hospital as she thinks wrist broken. She ordered an ambulance to take me to Glangwili. Didn't call as I know you're up to your eyes. Will do when I can. Lucky it's left wrist so can still write and call you. DON'T WORRY SIS! I'm a big girl now and will be fine. Got my chair and Carys is with me, of course.

Jane's heart gallops. She rereads the note. In a police situation when facing a criminal, she is always calm but when it comes to Meg, she finds it so difficult. Her instinct is to dash to the hospital but she makes herself grab a couple of bags of crisps, a chocolate bar and a bottle of water as she's starving and thirsty. She always has some snacks in reserve for when work gets hectic. She brings them with her as she forces herself to take her time, returning to the car and driving within the speed limit into Carmarthen. She feels as though she has become her sister's mother.

She parks legally and walks to the A&E department as calmly as she can. She roams the hospital until she finally finds Meg with Carys. They're in a queue to collect some painkillers from the pharmacy.

Once she has seen her sister, Jane's panic subsides and relief takes over. She reprimands herself for being so silly. Meg is a grown-up with a good brain and, apart from her disablement, can look after herself.

'Wouldn't have mattered if it had been a leg.'

'So true. Are you starving, Meg?'

'No, no. Carys got us both some sandwiches and disgusting coffee from the canteen.'

'Good on you, Carys.'

'Try my best, always try my best,' coos Carys.

When they began to cope with the horror of the train crash disaster, the sisters developed their own method of sending stress packing by making light of everything. Jane had being strong thrust upon her and has managed extraordinarily well. But the pain of what happened and how much of her sister's young life, as well as part of her own, has been stolen from them, remains in her sore heart. She misses both her parents but in particular her mother, as she is certain Meg does.

It is at moments like these that she longs for that practical, down-to-earth woman to walk in and take over. Their parents are a subject the sisters cannot jest about so instead of talking about them, they leave it alone. When they find themselves talking about their childhood, there is always the loss of their kind, reliable mum in the background to sour those memories.

Jane drives Meg, her chair in the boot and Carys sitting in the back. They arrive back at the bungalow at 9.15pm.

All of them are exhausted, but when they get home, Jane opens and heats a tin of soup for them and then helps Meg to bed. She finally falls into her own by 10.30pm. To get to Fishguard for 8am tomorrow she must allow a good hour, so she sets her alarm for 6.10am.

Meg has happily persuaded her to wake her, just help her to the loo, then leave her in her chair in her dressing gown and slippers. The washing and dressing can wait until Carys appears later.

Jane is physically, mentally and emotionally worn out. It's been a very long day.

22

8 JANUARY 2018. FISHGUARD

It turns out that PC Thomas has overlooked a vital factor. The man who deals with technological matters back in Carmarthen has announced there is no SIM card in the mobile phone found at the Cauldron. Jane is annoyed with Thomas. It's fundamental to check for a SIM card before taking a device back for inspection. She calls and ticks him off firmly.

'So very sorry, ma'am.' He draws out the r in very and the o in sorry. 'My bad, my bad.'

For the moment that lead has fizzled. If they could find the SIM, it could be an important help. Jane's heart is not happy that she must send more men up there to that freezing, dangerous place and ask them once again to comb the site looking for a tiny piece of plastic in the extremely unlikely event that it might be there. It is probably far away but just in case, literally every blade of grass on the top of the Cauldron must be examined with scrupulous care – and then she has an idea. Metal detectors. A strong enough detector should find it with relative ease. So she sets the operation in motion.

Now, she sits with Evans in her office chair and they brainstorm about the case. Evans bites the nail off a second finger and while Jane avoids watching him to stem any exasperation, he says, 'If Bette Davies jumped to her end, the last thing on her mind would have been her phone, surely? So this must point to a deliberate act by someone other than the drowned woman.' He pauses. 'Or does it? If it contained incriminating evidence against either herself or someone she wanted to protect, it is possible she thought of getting rid of it before jumping.'

'Good point, Evans.' Jane was immediately reminded that in spite of his annoying habits, Evans could think logically and well. She felt bad for allowing herself to be exasperated by him. He was a good man, at the end of the day. 'Except, thinking about it, Mike Hanson was apparently there so it's more probable that he grabbed it from her and deliberately removed the SIM then threw it away, dropping the empty phone before they departed. There were likely to be incriminating messages on it that Mike had sent her, so if it was him who dropped it, he wouldn't have meant to leave the SIM there.'

'Or, was Bette holding the phone and about to ring someone when her murderer wrenched it from her before pushing her off? Did they then remove the SIM and throw it somewhere other than the phone case?' Evans' latter explanation makes good sense. Especially as it had snowed around that time.

'There's a third possibility.' Evans' cogs were whirring now. 'That whoever killed her wanted us to find the phone.'

They agree that both seem the most likely theories they have come up with so far.

The DNA from the hair and toothbrushes has been analysed and the brown hair is a match for the remains of blood spatters on the dead woman's coat. The saltwater has done its best to remove them but the sharp-eyed Max has found a tiny spot remaining. This links Mike's blood to his partner's coat.

Jane talks this over with Evans and her chief superintendent but they cannot come up with a probable scenario. The best they can surmise is that Bette put up a fight before she was pushed to her death and managed somehow to scratch or cut her killer. With what they cannot tell and there was no sign of a knife or weapon with which she might have done this. Perhaps she just had sharp nails. If so, they have disintegrated in the water so there is no point asking Max if there's any skin or blood under them.

A call comes in from headquarters. A SIM card has been found up on the path by the Cauldron, close to where the phone was discovered. It is in the kiosk now and Jane will soon know whether it is Bette's.

When the technicians establish it to be so, Jane catches her breath. That it is still working is a miracle. Apparently, it was found under a crisp packet wrapper that had been frozen to the ground. For once a litterbug had been helpful. This could be the lucky breakthrough they need.

Jane is delighted to hear the news and shares her theory with Evans.

'I think whoever killed her intended to throw the SIM into the sea, but I believe the wind caught it and blew it back onto the land.'

She asks one of the technicians to bring the phone and SIM to Fishguard straight away.

While Jane is waiting for the tech guy to arrive, she has a chance to look through Bette's thick diary. The young woman comes across as a kind, intelligent person who loved Mike deeply and was distraught by the loss of her baby. It seems the couple's devotion was ruined by the tragedy and that things between them went downhill thereafter. Jane is particularly interested in a passage written on October 6th in 2017 where Bette's loneliness comes across clearly due to Mike having turned against her. She describes his hatred of her and conjectures whether he may plan to 'do away with' – but doesn't finish the sentence as it is too painful to write. She describes meeting Sara for the first time as a tonic to a friendless soul.

Jane learnt early in her career that you must just make a decision. You won't get them all right, but you have to make a decision or you won't move the investigation on. There are so many routes she could take but she decides to go with this one. The finger is pointing firmly at Mike. So, where has the man got to?

About two hours later, the tech man reaches the town hall; together he and Jane check through all the recent calls, messages and contacts. They prove Sara's story of the friendship between the two women. And they prove the problems between Mike and Bette, who seem to avoid speaking to one another when they can send curt texts instead. They also find some downright nasty texts swapped between Bette and Mike. They search for pictures but can see they've recently been deleted and are untraceable. Maybe among them had been photos of the baby that Bette couldn't bear to keep.

There is no proof but given the evidence they have plus the fact that there is no trace of Michael Hanson, the police now alter his status from a 'person of interest' to 'wanted for murder'. They put out an all-ports warning and posters are printed of his picture and circulated to all forces in the UK.

10 January 2018, Fishguard

And then, a couple of days later when all searches for Mike and his car have led nowhere, the Cardigan Police receive a call from a local farmer who reports what appears to be an abandoned blue BMW on a remote corner of his land at Foel Hendre near St Dogmaels. It has been left close to a headland on top of 500-foot cliffs. The only way it could have got there was down a private farm track and then across some rocky land. Apparently, the car has been noticed there for a couple of days but since the farmer had not had cause to go down recently, it might have been there since Christmas.

Jane hears about this and her heart jumps. She and Evans race to the spot. The number plate is quickly checked and found to belong to Michael Hanson. The car is empty but for a tartan scarf. Men and women wearing face masks and latex gloves check through it for traces of anything that might give them a clue but there is no blood, no sign of struggle, nothing to indicate any violence has taken place.

They go over the bodywork and take photographs of everything but there is nothing in there. Fingerprint experts are called to the car. It is carefully dusted and the scarf is bagged up. The glove compartment and the side pockets are emptied and the contents bagged up as well and the lot is taken back to Llangunnor.

The ground around the car is thoroughly searched. The track is studied for tyre prints but the snow has been their enemy. The land is high and there are still some frozen patches of snow and no footprints. Careful scrutiny finds some scattered brown polyester as well as some blue fibres on the ground between the car and the cliff edge. Later analysis reveals the brown to be from a coat or puffer jacket; and the blue from jeans.

By the edge they find a pair of man's size-ten, brown walking boots, lying haphazardly on their sides as though hurriedly unlaced and kicked off.

For a moment Jane wishes remote areas like this had CCTV. She decides the best course is to arrange for a couple of police drones to be sent over the edge of the cliff and down to the inaccessible strip of pebble beach below.

It is half a day before this happens but when the cameras carefully scan every inch of the spot, they find no sign of any disturbance or a body.

If someone jumped or was pushed, their body would have been carried out to sea on the tide.

Jane sits at a table with Evans and three other detectives on the case. Unfortunately, they have no timeline. The farmer said he had not been down to that area since Christmas so the car could have been there for over two weeks. Three sets of DNA have been found in the car. Some match those from the toothbrushes and the hairs taken from the bedroom in Cliff Edge as well as Sara's who stated she had got into Mike's car when she tried to reason with him not to drive in a snow blizzard.

Deciding to presume that Mike Hanson drove the car to the cliff edge, the group discuss the fibres found on the ground. For what possible reason would the man have crawled to the edge leaving behind fibres from his clothing? Might instead he have been dragged or pulled? On second thoughts, did he drag himself? This could only have been because he had been too weak to stand or he had collapsed for some reason.

'Or' – Evans puts up his hand like a schoolboy in class – 'did he drug himself out of his head in order to be certain to die?'

The team comes up with a predictive list of possible scenarios.

Option One: Mike Hanson committed suicide by jumping off the cliff.

Option Two: He abandoned his car there to make it seem that way. He deliberately left a pair of walking boots then walked a long way (presumably wearing a different pair of boots or shoes) to the nearest place he could get food and transport and make a getaway.

Option Three: Same as Two except that someone helped him get away and that someone is most likely to be Sara de

Vries. Might she have driven her car to the nearest parking place and waited while he set the scene by dragging himself across the ground to the edge in order to leave evidence? Then he walked to her waiting car so she could drive him to make his escape.

If that were the case, it was likely those two were romantically involved. So, did Mike murder Bette on his own or did the two together plot to kill her? If the latter, then Sara knows a great deal more than she has been telling them.

They decide to discount Option Two since, although it might have been a clever plan for a clever man to come up with, there has been a major manhunt for him and no trace has showed up. Someone somewhere would have spotted him, sold food to him, given him a lift or seen him on public transport.

So they are left with Mike killing himself or being killed. But by whom?

They definitely need to bring Sara in for questioning again.

Trying a different angle, Jane wonders whether Sara had some sexual relationship with either the male or the female. She has nothing to lose by trying to goad a reaction.

'Did you find Mike attractive, Sara?' Jane fixes a deep gaze on her and watches the woman warily.

'I think you are trying to catch me out, Inspector. I was not having an affair with him if that's what you're getting at. I was not even contemplating such a thing and never would. He was all right though. Yes, I suppose he was attractive in a way, but I never considered it as he was my friend's partner and I am not the type to allow such a thing to cross my mind.'

'Fair enough. Do you think he fancied you?' Jane half smiles in recognition of their game of cat and mouse.

This time, Jane thinks she sees the hint of a blush tint Sara's cheeks.

'Certainly not. No, of course he didn't, no.'

A raw nerve has been touched, it seems.

But however hard Jane tries, she gets nowhere. Sara is not going to give. So she tries another tack. 'Then, perhaps, Bette was more to your liking?'

Now Sara demurs. 'You're going too far, Inspector Owen. I am not that type.'

'You mean, you don't contemplate women as sexual partners?'

'No, I most emphatically do not.'

Jane wonders why she protests so much and thinks of the lady's insincere overacting in *Hamlet*'s play within the play. Maybe she's a closet lesbian. She prods away on this line for a while longer but gets nowhere fast. Sara is a quick learner and has altered from super-helpful to someone who now feels trapped and is turning super-difficult. Whatever Jane tries, however many insincerities she thinks she has extracted from Sara, she gets nowhere nearer to who killed Bette Davies and/or Mike Hanson. She and the team keep coming back to the same old problem. There simply is no tangible evidence and nothing to go on except Sara's word, reliable or unreliable as it may be.

The main part of the investigation is now moved back to Llangunnor. With no witnesses, no actual evidence and nothing to go on but what they have been told, all they can hope for is to find Mike Hanson.

The case has led to nothing but dead ends and although there is no trace of him, Mike is still wanted for the murder. No living relatives have come forward, so the police go ahead and arrange Bette's funeral. The death of Bette Davies becomes a cold case.

. . .

19 January 2018, Llangunnor

A call comes into the station that a female body has been found by a man walking his dog by woodland on the side of a small lane near a place called Porthyrhyd. There has been a recent partial thaw although there are still pockets of snow and ice on the ground in places.

The half-frozen corpse is brought to Max Granger who can tell that it has been iced up for some time where it was lying on the ground in what was probably a large snow drift.

There are no marks of violence on the body or any incriminating evidence to suggest she was taken there, but it has snowed quite a lot since the time she went missing and it is clear she has been there for at least two, maybe three weeks. On account of the cold conditions the body is perfectly preserved.

There are no tyre tracks or other signs of wrongdoing to be found.

The puzzle is why is she there and why is her coat lying beside her? The first is explained by the fact that she may have been overcome by cold, as she was not wearing clothing for walking far in the snowy weather conditions in early January.

Max's explanation for her coat lying beside her was that twenty to fifty per cent of hypothermia deaths are associated with 'paradoxical undressing'.

When Jane asks him about this, he says, 'Your body responds to cold by constricting blood vessels, stopping warm blood from getting cooled at the extremities. But in hypothermia, the body becomes exhausted fighting the cold and the tiny muscles holding the blood vessels closed tire out. The blood vessels open up and blood rushes back to the skin causing a hot flush, which makes the person tear off their clothing.' He flips over the page of his report and looks at Jane before he continues. She can feel herself blushing. There is something so charming about the way he looks at her. She thinks she spots a glimmer of amusement in his eyes when he says, 'Of course, it could simply be because in this case the brain was so disorientated that it decided it was really hot, so the lady started to discard her clothing, increasing, therefore, the rate of heat loss.'

Having originally presumed it might turn out to be a case of looking at the brain and finding dementia or Alzheimer's, on close examination Max found some sticky substance on the lips, nose, cheeks and hair and also on her wrists. It seems the poor woman had her wrists and mouth bound with insulating or duct tape. The tape was then removed. Perhaps in the hope that it would look like what Max first thought it might be.

But it has turned out to be murder.

DNA tests have established that it is Gwyneth Edwards, the woman missing from Moylegrove.

The body is nearer Swansea, though, so Gwyneth Edwards' son, Aled is the first person they look at.

The first thing to establish is what might he gain from his mother's death. Evans checks the worth of her cottage in Moylegrove which is about £140,000 – but the place could be rented during the high season for up to £700 per week. Quite a motive. From their earlier interviews, they know he is comparatively poor. They know he works at a factory on the northern outskirts of Swansea, so Jane calls him and asks for the address there. He gives it to her and asks if there's some news of his mother and she says there is and that she is coming to talk to him as soon as possible. He sounds extremely anxious.

Jane takes Evans, PC Roberts and another constable to the factory where Aled helps assemble electronics on a production line. They ask at reception for the manager to speak to them. They explain that they have found the mother of Aled Edwards and that it looks likely she may have been murdered. They ask for a quiet room where they can break the news to Aled and interview him. The manager complies, allows them to use his office and disappears off to the assembly line to find Aled and bring him to them.

They stand as Jane breaks the news to him and he covers his face with his hands, sinks into an armchair and blubs. 'Oh no! Not Mam!'

They give him some time.

'I'm so sorry to break this news to you, Aled.' Jane clears her throat. 'What is very much worse is that it looks like she was murdered.'

'*Murdered?*' He is incredulous. His hands drop from his face. He wipes his eyes. 'Murdered? But how? Why? I mean who would murder her? Mother? For what possible reason?' He seems genuinely upset, but then they all do.

'I am so sorry, Aled but we are going to have to ask you to accompany us to the station at Llangunnor as we need you to identify the body and ask you a few more questions.'

The sobbing man stands up. 'She was all I had left. My dad drowned, my wife left me, I hardly see my daughter and now Mother. I can't bear it, I can't bear it.' He looks like a broken man. But Jane doesn't feel sorry for the man who only seems to feel sorry for himself, not his poor mother who must have known terrible fear and suffering.

Jane watches Aled like an eagle when he sees his mother's body and he seems deeply upset. She, Evans and Roberts drive the heartbroken man back to the Gelli Rhedyn development at Fforestfach near the M4, over three miles north of Swansea.

'Mind if we come in, Aled? We'd just like to have a look around where your Mum spent her last days. All right?'

'That's okay.'

Aled leads them into a slightly grubby, cramped two-bed flat that smells of cooking oil and is in need of redecorating. The single bedroom door is open and as they pass, they see a child's room with a few tired toys on a shelf. Jane recalls that his wife left him some time ago and that his child visits only from time to time. He is polite and offers them some tea which they decline. They find nothing and leave the man to grieve alone.

Meanwhile, tests show Aled's fingerprints on his mother's coat and handbag and in spite of his strong denials, some duct tape is found in his flat and it is seen that he has been 'borrowing' money from his hard-up mother.

The autopsy reveals a large quantity of sleeping pills in the victim's stomach and it turns out that the son has an almost finished packet of the very same drug, widely prescribed by doctors. Although the evidence is circumstantial, there is a great deal of it. Aled is arrested and brought to trial for matricide. The jury are not out for long, the crown prosecutor having made a far stronger case than the defence. The jury returns a verdict of guilty of murder in the first degree. Given a full life sentence with a minimum term of twenty years for what the judge describes as a 'thoroughly evil, cruel and despicable act,' still swearing his innocence, Aled Edwards is sent away to prison for a long time.

There is great celebration in the police station at Llangunnor and Jane is clapped and cheered when she gets back to the office. So this has turned out to be her first solved murder case after all, the Bette Davies case having gone cold.

23

FEBRUARY 2019. DURRUM CASTLE, SCOTLAND

The best memory is the one I'd been building up to all that time where I'd had to feign friendship with that awful woman and achieved it with such ease. What a silly bitch, thinking Mike had loved her when he had clearly not. It had been me – not her – he had loved. No doubt about it.

Losing that child has turned out to be the very best thing. Where would I be now if things had been otherwise? I remember the fearful argument that shook the rafters of Cliff Edge and how he had started yelling and screaming that he had researched into newspaper archives and discovered Bethan had stolen her parents' life savings of £38,000, run away and changed her name. He had left Cliff Edge in a black rage. I can almost feel the cold as I ran out after him into the dark. It was snowing a blizzard and he jumped into his car ready to drive off. I remember standing without my coat, freezing in the dark in front of his car, begging him to calm down.

Finally, he had agreed to come back into the house. Even then, I had been able to push the right buttons to win the man around.

We agreed that the following day we would drive up to

Cemaes Bay to see whether there was a way to resolve the trouble.

I must admit to a shiver of enjoyment that I persuaded him to believe me. It is a delightful memory, the getting him to agree to drive us to his favourite spot and try to recapture the wonder he had felt on seeing it for the first time the previous year. At breakfast the following morning, I made him a large mug of extra strong coffee and a couple of his favourite poached eggs.

But when he had driven us there, I let him have it. Just how stupid was that to leave those sexy texts on his phone. It is making me angry now to recall that message coming through on his mobile when he was in the shower:

Mike I am desperate. Please, please, I need to talk to you urgently. I'll be in Cam Café between 12-1 today. x

Pathetic! I suppose she was going to tell him she'd miscarried. What could the man have possibly done about that? Honestly!

I, of course, deleted that text and went myself to Cam Café. How simple to follow her from there to where she lived, trail her for a couple of days and what luck to discover she had a collie and where she generally walked it. Now I had the perfect excuse to talk to her. From there, it was a doddle. I gleaned as much as I could about the slag shagging my man.

And I've got to hand it to him, Mike was a good lover. He had a high sex drive like me and was an attentive man who always made sure I orgasmed before him... But how very dare he fuck someone other than me? How DARE he? He'd adored me and all along had been fucking someone else.

Because I had been pregnant, that wet excuse for a man had been so worried to do anything that might damage the baby, he had barely touched me throughout the pregnancy. It wasn't as if

I'd ever wanted the wretched child anyway but I had had to relent to his insistence.

In sight of him and others, I was great at the role of doting mother, but when that man wasn't around, I would shut all the doors and keep away from the wretched child who did nothing but cry. A few times, I was so fed up with it that I went out and left it screaming in its cot.

Going back through his messages, I found quite a few others he had failed to delete. It hadn't been hard to work out that he'd been screwing the bitch for ages. What a moron he'd been not to get rid of all those stupid, soppy texts.

God, I so enjoyed seeing their faces when they saw each other at Cliff Edge. Mike did a half-reasonable job of hiding it but she – she just went to pieces! I had thought she would. Brilliant!

Before I killed him, I told Mike how easy it had been to track down his girlfriend and to befriend her. I whispered to him as he had become groggier, how easy it would be to lure that fucking bitch to the Cauldron and push her over the cliff edge to where the witches belong.

Mike's driving became increasingly erratic as he drove us down the track to that remote place by the hugely high cliffs. By the time he had parked up near the edge, where there wasn't a soul for miles around, he'd started to become very sleepy.

I sat in the car waiting for him to slip into unconsciousness – those sleeping pills the doctor had prescribed worked really well in the coffee. I think it was nine I added, crushed, of course. The strong coffee had disguised their taste.

I got a heavy torch found in the glove compartment, dragged him out of his treasured car and hit him over the head with all the strength I had.

Over and over again I smashed his head until a gaping crack had appeared in the skull and I could see the membrane that covers the brain. There was a lot of blood on the snow; pretty colours.

After checking to ensure his pulse had gone, and that his phone was in his pocket, I lugged and dragged him to the edge where I rolled him over it. I took off his boots to leave clues for the police. It took a major effort but it was so worth it to watch him fall like a lead weight before he smacked into the sea. Dropping 500 feet, a body makes a huge splash as it hits the waves, causing a high spume of seawater and sending a massive spray into the air. I watched it turn into a small cyclone of water that revolved violently around the sinking man before he ended on the seabed. I was sure he had gone out far enough to remain out of sight in his sea grave and not to reappear when the tide went out. Once he had been in the water a while, the lungs would fill up with air to more than twice their usual size and the body would be buoyant. But by then, the currents would have taken over.

Before I left, I took out a spade from the boot Mike kept in case the car got stuck in a snowdrift or mud and although the ground was almost frozen, I managed to chip away at it to disturb it enough to bury as much of the blood as I could and the rest I shovelled into an old hessian sack (thank you, painstaking Mr Mike Hanson) kept to put under the tyres for extra grip in the event they got stuck in icy snow.

I walked away from the car confident more snow would cover my tracks. It was tough to leave such a lovely car. It was worth a lot of money and I racked my brain to think how I could keep it. But once the police started looking for Mike it would be high on their search list. So, I had to harden my heart and leave that shiny BMW where it was. I walked away and back to Cliff Edge. Walking back along the coastal path, into the ocean went the spade and the sack into which I had shoved my blood-spattered gloves and the torch. When I had got home, I had told my 'friend' that after a long talk, darling Mike had insisted he went back to Cambridge and that the two of us should stay until we wanted to leave. I told her he'd dropped me off before heading home.

This had rattled the bitch, who had tried to hide it, but I could tell. But no more had been said until the next day up by the Cauldron. Then, and oh what fun that was, I let that fucking whore in on just how much I had known.

A week before the police had arrived at Cliff Edge, which I'd made sure of by tipping them off, I ordered some nitrile gloves online. I wore them all the time while I swapped the framed photo for one of him and the whore together at Christmas. I'd got it printed by an online company and sized to fit the frame she'd given us and it had come back in good time. Of course, the frame had her DNA on it. I was particularly pleased with myself for that idea.

And also, still wearing the gloves, what a brainwave to leave the hair in the bed and the toothbrush in their bathroom. Knowing the police would be thorough, I swapped all my own possessions from my room to hers. Testament to my fine character was the diary with all those soppy entries as an extra bit of insurance.

All those thrillers I had read in the summer came in handy.

At Cliff Edge earlier, before we set out to visit the Cauldron, I'd deliberately dropped my phone on the floor and the whore had bent to pick it up. The police would test it for fingerprints, so that was covered. I wanted it to look as though someone had tried to get rid of the SIM but left it near enough the phone for the police to find. They might test the SIM for prints too so before they had left, I used a pair of eyebrow tweezers to extract it from the phone case. It had been inserted by the phone shop when I bought the mobile and I had never removed it until that moment. Without touching it, I placed it carefully in an envelope and pocketed it in the coat I wore that day. I knew the police would comb the place for clues. After the whore had gone over the edge, I dropped her phone and tipped the SIM out of its envelope a few yards away. I wanted the cops to read it so to protect it from the weather I used a bit of litter to cover it and partially hid it with snow. I knew the cops would see, pick up the packet and find the SIM underneath.

A few days before, I engineered a conversation with the whore about how difficult it is to remember all the different passwords and the stupid slag had given me just what I'd been after: 'Oh, I keep mine in a file on my laptop!' So all I had to do was watch and learn her laptop password.

I remember the triumphant moment when I shoved her from behind. To avoid getting DNA on her clothes, I used the point of the trekking pole.

What a moment, seeing her plunge into the Cauldron. So satisfying to watch her struggle in the freezing water unable to get out. It gives me goosebumps of pleasure and a great feeling of invincibility to know she suffered in that sea grave, even if it wasn't for long. No less than she deserved and she certainly felt great fear.

I cannot help congratulating myself on my own brilliance in persuading her to wear my green puffer coat on that last walk of hers. I assured her it was so much warmer than the cheap one she had. The stupid slag had failed to notice the few blood spatters of Mike's, but had she done so, I had a ready answer about helping a poor injured deer I had found on the road. The goodie-goodie bitch would love a story like that. I always kept an extra puffer at Cliff Edge that I was now wearing. But Bette was known in the neighbourhood for wearing that particular green coat so if the police checked with anyone local, I'd covered that one. And if they found the blood spatters... then they might jump to the conclusion that Bette had killed Mike.

That cleaning woman had to go. I'd forgotten about her until she showed up. So, I let her tidy and then improvised. So glad I'd bought that box of nitrile gloves, I got a pair out and put them on. I then got some broad duct tape that we kept in the toolbox, I then cut two suitable lengths of duct tape and put them ready on the back of one of the kitchen chairs.

I sat the unsuspecting woman down, made her a cup of tea and as I brought it to her, from behind her chair I grabbed her arms, forced them behind her back and quickly taped her wrists together. That done, it was simple to tape her mouth.

I needed her to be able to breathe through her nose for the moment, so I made her leave the table, walk out of the house in the falling snow to the car and forced her to lie down in the boot. I threw her coat and bag and the suitcase she'd brought in, after her and took the duct tape and a pair of scissors with me. She had to remain alive for the moment. Then I drove her to a place where there was a lot of snow near the outskirts of Swansea. I needed to cast the son as the likely murderer.

I got the shivering woman out of the boot and taped her nose as well so she couldn't breathe at all then I made her walk into a deep drift. I watched her collapse and waited a minute or so until she lost consciousness and was on the way out, then I untaped her hands, mouth and nose, threw her coat and bag down beside her and left her there. The snow would cover my tracks and was already partially covering her freezing body. In the morning I chucked the suitcase, the duct tape and the gloves in the sea.

So the last one was gone and that was that.

All except the darling dogs and they're the ones I loved. Once the police allowed me to leave Cliff Edge, I drove home to Sara's dingy, horrible flat where I had to wait with the dogs until things died down. I must say I played an award-winning perfor-mance being that woman. I got the accent just right with just that hint of foreign that one isn't quite sure of where the person comes from and that careful way of speaking and even her gushing over-the-top politeness.

But after a month I made a bolt for it and the three of us headed for London. We drove away in my new estate car with my new licence, courtesy of Sara de Vries. I managed to keep quite a bit of Mike's money. In fact, I had hidden away a decent sum in readiness for this occasion.

At Christmas, I'd transferred £20,000 from the joint account into Sara's as a 'gift.' Of course, the police had checked my bank details as they had seen the transfer and when they'd asked about it, I said it had been a loan from my friend Bette to help me through a financially sticky time. Clever, so clever, I cannot help be so pleased with all my planning and the way it worked out so well.

I had a bank card that drew money from Sara's measly account. I had her national insurance number and her easily copied signature and – at last – I had a passport!

When I moved to London, I changed my name by deed poll to Jackie London. Jackie after Onassis. Quite a role model, I thought. I dyed my hair black to match. London seemed a good enough name.

I had to put the dogs in temporary kennels in Kensington while I rented a bedsit for eight weeks. I walked them every day for a couple of hours or more and that is where I met Donald.

So Bette Davies is no more. And nor is Sara de Vries. I have killed them both off. I am young, I am desirable and I know just how effective my pulling power can be. I am resourceful. I am versatile. I am imaginative, entrepreneurial, clever, a highly convincing liar. I am a player. I can have any man I want. And I am getting bolder as time goes by.

This will be the third time I have reinvented myself.

It may not be the last.

6 February 2020. Durrum Castle, Perthshire. Lady Jackie McNarris' Five-Year Diary.

So here begins my diary as the newly-married wife of Sir Donald McNarris of Durrum Castle in Perthshire. We have just returned from the most romantic fortnight's honeymoon in Sri Lanka and I must be the happiest woman alive. We went exploring inland which was fantastic. What an amazing country. Such lovely people. I was the only tall, dark-haired, blue-eyed young woman some of them had ever seen. It was a wonderful place although the climate proved a bit too humid and the food a bit too spicy for poor Donald.

We had a few nights in our Kensington house before coming back here where we have settled in with Brynn and Gin and Donald's darling Labradors with whom my two have a great time. This is the most beautiful countryside with forests, mountains, glens and the river Tay very nearby in which the dogs love to swim and Donald to fly-fish for salmon. It is great hiking country.

The castle is very well run by the staff and apart from talking about the menus and to the housekeeper about guests, I shan't have to worry too much, which is great.

Donald is at the age when he's had enough galivanting to be happy to stay here and let me visit our house in Kensington whenever I like as I do love London. Also, he has children and grandchildren, some of whom are grown up, so he has no interest in having more kids. What a great man I have found.

How lucky to have met him in Hyde Park walking his Labradors (he takes them everywhere with him). Especially lucky, since he only goes to London about twice a year to visit his sister who also lives in Kensington. Our courtship went slowly to begin with: we were both scared of the big age gap but once he had invited me to Durrum and had seen how I had taken to it like a duck to water, I think something clicked for both of us.

His previous wife died late last year. I read about it in the papers at the time: she was killed in a horrific motorway pile-up on the M6. Poor Donald was miserable. But I am happy to say I have brought some happiness back into his life which he deserves.

His children don't seem to approve but I shall win them around in time. I do understand their reluctance. I'm younger than all of them! Jealous, I expect and maybe they think it's too soon. Well, they should think about their father and what makes him happy.

EPILOGUE

A t Cable Bay in Aberffraw, on Anglesey Island off North
Wales, over thousands of years sand has been blown
inland by onshore winds to form extensive dunes that roll
parallel to the strip of beach.

It is the first rain-free day for eight days running and a pale,
weak sun has appeared in a whitish sky. This is enough for the
local kids on holiday. When the weather is right and the usually
aggressive wind speeds are calmed, their chosen pastime is
beach frisbee. There is always a breeze blowing in off the sea but
that is part of the fun.

One of the older boys executes a throw so vigorous that the
frisbee, caught on the breeze is carried high into the air and sails
inland to float down among the dunes. Children scramble
through the sand to search for it. When one stumbles on something hard and stubs her toe, she stops to see what she has
tripped on and shrieks in shock. Half buried in the sand, among
the coarse grass, the grinning jawbone and lower half of a
human face juts out.

On April 17th, 2020, in a laboratory in Anglesey, a forensic
scientist closely studies the skull which is attached to the upper

part of a spine that was found at Cable Bay. She cannot miss the depressions and fractures on the top and back of the skull that, judging from its size, is definitely male, and has been hit by a hard object several times. She concludes there is no doubt that the man was murdered. DNA tests come back to match with missing person, Michael Hanson.

Summer 2020, Carmarthen

DCI Jane Owen is watching the news, cuddled in the arms of Gareth on his sofa in his Carmarthen house. These days, life for Jane is so much easier.

Meg now drives, she has a job in Carmarthen and has even reunited with her original boyfriend who is staying with her in the Llangunnor bungalow tonight.

These days, Jane doesn't feel that constant pressure all the time. Her job is not easy and demands long hours but she doesn't mind that. Before, there was all that extra worry and work involved with Meg.

The headline on the local news is that missing suspected murderer Michael Hanson's skull had been found on the beach at Cable Bay.

Jane sits up, rigid with interest. She had missed this earlier as it was her weekend off. She asks Gareth sweetly if they can turn down the volume while she thinks about this. He knows it was her case and has done it before she's finished the question. She leans back on the sofa and looks out of the window. The dark sky helps her think.

Can it be that a murderer has been murdered? Or was perhaps Mike Hanson not a murderer after all? She wonders whether there is a chance she was duped by Sara de... *What was the woman called?* She wonders whether, after all, the woman killed Mike and pushed Bette Davies.

But what had she hoped to gain? Money? No. Could jealousy have been a strong enough motive? Jane's brain whirred. Did she check out Sara de whatnot properly? Her background, her love life, her character? She knows she didn't do nearly as much as she should have done. She concentrated the enquiry wholly on Mike Hanson. She had been so certain he was to blame.

She remembers the abandoned BMW and quite out of the blue, a memory comes to her of Sara saying she had sat in the car with Mike Hanson and begged him not to drive in a snow-storm. Jane thinks back long and hard. Sara's DNA was in the BMW. *She* could have pushed Mike over the cliff.

She now also begins to wonder whether she put away the right man for the murder of Gwyneth Edwards who cleaned for the people at Cliff Edge. She had never considered that Sara might have done away with her too. Perhaps because she had seen too much? It would be a plausible reason. Guilt runs through her and she shudders. Did she get it wrong in one or even both cases? Her first two murder cases – should she reopen them? It wouldn't look great on her record...

THE END

Printed in Great Britain
by Amazon